THE GOLDEN CLASP

Paris, France, 1789

Dear Armand,

I am so afraid. Death lurks in every corner. If you were with me, nothing could harm us . . .

Armand, are you hiding something from me? I love you, yet feel I know nothing about you. But I want to know you, more than anything . . .

When this region of terror ends, I pray we will find each other. Until then, I fear for us both . . .

Emma

Point R♥mance

THE
GOLDEN CLASP

Clare Frances Holmes

Complete and Unabridged

spectrum
LARGE PRINT

First published in Great Britain in 1998 by
Scholastic Children's Books
London

First Large Print Edition
published 2000
by arrangement with
Scholastic Children's Books
London

British Library CIP Data

Holmes, Clare Frances
The golden clasp.—Large print ed.—
(Point romance)—Spectrum imprint
1. France—History—Revolution,
1789 – 1799 —Fiction
2. Love stories
3. Young adult fiction
4. Large type books
I. Title
823.9′14 [J]

ISBN 0–7089–9529–2

Published by
F. A. Thorpe (Publishing)
Anstey, Leicestershire

Set by Words & Graphics Ltd.
Anstey, Leicestershire
Printed and bound in Great Britain by
T. J. International Ltd., Padstow, Cornwall

This book is printed on acid-free paper

1

'What to do with you, I do not know!' cried Emma's stepmother. 'I take pains to make you a young lady, but you thwart me at every turn!

'You like nothing but to roam the countryside, walk, run, climb trees. Scarcely the behaviour of a young lady with a professor for a father, and who lives in the Bell House!'

The year was 1788, and at this time Emma was fifteen, tall and slim, with fly-away auburn hair and grey eyes. She moved swiftly, with a grace all her own, but none of this pleased Stepmamma.

Emma had not expected her father to marry again, but he had attended a conference, and from there had returned unexpectedly with a bride.

Mrs Kent, as she would always be known, was stout, with a pale, flat face, and a frizz of light-brown hair. Her one idea in life was to enter what she termed society — and take her new family with her.

'We must be concerned for Emma's future,' Mrs Kent said. 'She is now marriageable material, and the time is swiftly approaching when she must be prepared to receive suitors and make a choice.'

The professor was a tall, handsome man of around forty. He became evasive about this matter of Emma's future.

'Emma has been a wonderful daughter to me. She keeps the notes of my lectures, lists the students at the university, sees to my bills — generally keeps my affairs in order.'

'That is all to the good,' Mrs Kent replied. 'But something more is required at the present time.'

She coaxed Emma's father round, and in no time at all Mademoiselle Yvette arrived from France and entered the household at the Bell House.

'This will improve the tone of everything here!' Mrs Kent cried. 'For Emma and the whole establishment lack polish, discernment and style!'

It was one of the best things Mrs Kent had ever done.

Mamselle bounced into the Bell House full of gaiety and a kind of uncritical affection. She loved everyone and everyone loved her. She gave no offence, and saw none. She swept through the rather staid home like a breeze from the wilds of Provence.

She was small in stature, with dark hair in natural ringlets and a clear skin. When she was settled, she clapped her hands and cried: 'French is the language of this house from now on!

'By Christmas, everyone must speak French like a native! Come now, no more English is spoken here. Emma, conjugate these verbs! And Madame, read aloud from this play by Molière.'

Mamselle Yvette also set about improving the posture of Emma and her neighbourhood friends. 'Walk around the room with a book on your head! Curtsy low, but don't fall down. Speak clearly. Do not gush. And now I will show you how to choose cordials and wines.'

It was after Christmas, when the cold gripped the country and ice formed on the fountain in the quad of St Jude's College in Cambridge, that, rubbing his chilblains, the Master of the College called Professor Blythe into his study.

'I have received a communication from

a high official in the government,' he began. 'They wish a young French gentleman to attend the college to take a course in English Literature, which is your subject, Professor, is it not? They also request that this young man should reside with an English family in order to perfect his knowledge of the English language. Could you accommodate him, Professor, at the Bell House?'

'I feel sure this could be arranged,' David Blythe answered. 'May I ask this future student's name?'

'I am afraid not. My source in the government stresses that this young man must be incognito. He will be known merely as Armand. My informant stressed that departure from France at this time is frowned upon. Almost forbidden. But the family of this young man wish him to perfect his education among us and so these private arrangements have been made.'

'I quite understand, and agree,' Professor Blythe replied. 'When may I expect my new student and house guest?'

'Almost immediately. He is due to arrive at the end of this week.'

When Mrs Kent knew that a foreign

4

student was to arrive, a gale of sweeping, dusting, washing and polishing took place. Somehow, Mrs Kent imagined that this unknown young man could lead them all, the whole family, into some dream she had of social success. Somehow, they were all going to enter high society.

When Armand stepped down from his carriage and entered the hall of the house, they saw that he was tall and slim. His hair had a chestnut sheen, his eyes were brown. He had a frank, open and pleasing smile.

He greeted each one in turn, bowing and murmuring pleasantries. He came at last to Emma, who had stood watching the proceedings of Armand's arrival.

'Mamselle Emma,' said Armand, and took Emma's hand. She looked at his face searchingly, for she wished to try to know the nature of the newcomer into their lives.

He is young; seventeen, she thought. But though not of mature years, there was about him an aura of steadiness, resolution, lack of fear. He would be a good man to have as a friend, Emma thought. Stalwart in defence, loyal and trustworthy.

But for now, she curtsied, as Mamselle had taught her and withdrew her hand.

Lizbeth, the housekeeper, arrived to take Armand's luggage and after he had visited his room upstairs, they all went into supper.

* * *

Armand, of course, had his classes to attend at the university with Professor Blythe. But he seemed to have a fair amount of free time, which he spent at the Bell House.

So Emma and Armand went out together, walking through the lanes and byways of Little Marlowe, the village where Emma lived. They went further afield, through the surrounding country-side, across meadows, farmlands, through forests and dales. They talked, they laughed, they teased each other. Their silences were companionable, and perhaps said more than words.

It was a time of happiness for Emma; Armand seemed to match her thoughts and activities. He also seemed to relish the companionship with Emma. The whole household approved and liked the young Frenchman, whose family and background were unknown to them all.

Emma heard Armand and her father talking together one evening, after the meal was cleared. 'There are many injustices in France today,' the young man said. 'Poverty, oppression, exploitation. These ills have been borne by my countrymen for many years, but many say that the time is ripe for these inequalities to be removed.'

'By peaceful means only, I trust,' Emma's father answered in his calm and equable voice. 'Not by violence and illegal means. Not one drop of blood must be spilled to bring about these reforms, Armand. To resort to cruelty would make nonsense of your beliefs.'

Mamselle interposed herself at this point and Mrs Kent came in with coffee.

The professor also now indicated that Emma and Armand should proceed to the library. 'Please help Armand to select some books which will help him with his thesis. And it must be on English history, Armand, and not French!' Emma's father cried in a jocular way. Armand smiled in reply, their former slight disagreement quite forgotten. 'Mamselle will join you shortly.'

Armand took Emma's hand, and they

7

then left the sitting-room and entered the room which was Emma's favourite in the whole house.

A fire burned steadily in the grate, lighting up the rows of books, the desk and the easy chairs. The air seemed filled with a kind of pleasant expectancy.

Armand still held Emma's hand in his. 'Your hands are beautifully shaped, Emma. And you yourself have a special kind of attractiveness and poise.'

This was the first time that any such compliment had been paid to Emma, and she was quite overwhelmed. But even more so when Armand raised her hand to his lips and kissed it lightly, but tenderly.

'We must choose your books!' cried Emma, trying to gain some composure.

'But I know enough for my essay,' Armand answered. 'Come and sit down. I wish to talk to you. I did not expect to find pleasure in England, Emma. I thought the country harsh and lacking in amenities. But in your household I have found happiness and true values. My stay here has been an experience I shall prize all my life.'

Emma was at a loss for words. But Armand resumed. 'When I return to

France, I must enrol in the Royal Military Academy of Paris. The knowledge I have gained here will help my service to my country.

'I love France. My country has my devotion. But my devotion, Emma, is now also placed elsewhere.'

Emma's face coloured, and she found she was gripping Armand's hand in her own.

'You have given me a rare taste of personal happiness, Emma. Something I did not expect, or could not foresee. Believe me, my attachment to you has taken me unawares. But I accept the strength of my feelings for you. I trust you also will accept the strength of your feelings for myself.'

Armand took Emma in his arms and kissed her with a sweet closeness. Emma responded to him and embraced him also. And so they sat entwined in the quietude of the library, before the fire which still burned with a glow of embers.

'When do you have to return to France?' Emma asked at last.

'Very soon now. Next week,' answered Armand. 'But I promise you, Emma, we shall meet again. I promise you we will not part for ever. Somehow, our paths will cross. Somehow, we shall meet and be together again.'

At this moment Mamselle entered the library, in search of a book she said to take to bed. She appeared to notice nothing unusual, smiled, bade Emma and Armand a goodnight and went away.

Armand escorted Emma to the door of her room, and bowed again over her hand. Emma went into her room and closed the door.

★ ★ ★

Emma lay in her bed, and contemplated the events of the evening.

She remembered Armand's words, the sincere expression of his face, the intent gaze of his eyes. He had told her his feelings, revealing his deep emotions. And she had responded to him in kind.

She remembered how she had flushed at his words; her whole body had seemed to have been on fire. His expressions of concern had warmed her lonely heart and mind and left a glow in her inner consciousness she never wanted to lose.

She got up out of bed, and looked out of the window at the trees, the lawn and the outline of the distant village. And he had to leave so soon! She felt that this parting would be grievous, indeed.

★　★　★

Armand left the Bell House early on a morning in March. All the family gathered in the hallway to see him off.

He bowed to everyone, and thanked them all warmly for their hospitality. He thanked also the professor for his instructions and the courses they had taken together. Emma gathered that Armand had done well and had been awarded a university diploma.

To Emma, Armand was formal, though she knew his feelings were deep, though hidden. But their hands clung together for a long time and his kiss upon her cheek was warm and very close.

Tears filled her eyes but she would not allow them to fall. They said goodbye at the door as Armand entered the carriage. Then they turned back indoors and resumed their lives.

But a mood of depression seemed to

11

grip the residents of the Bell House. The weather was cold and chilly, the sky overcast, threatening rain or snow. They all sought a diversion, but none came.

And then Mamselle Yvette received a letter from France. She took it upstairs to read in privacy and, when she came down, she addressed them all as they were assembled in the sitting-room.

'I have had a letter from my former employers, Count and Countess Duval, and they have requested that I should return to France to take up my duties with them again. Little Henri needs me, they write, and the Countess herself has some projects upon which she wishes my assistance.'

There was a murmur of dismay from the whole family as Mamselle told them her news, for Mamselle had become a well-regarded and appreciated addition to the household. Her loss would never be replaced.

But Mamselle was continuing: 'My employers have asked me to recommend to them a young English lady who could enter their château and give lessons in English and the English values and ways of life. She could travel back with me to

France, for I must leave shortly. Almost forthwith.

'The young person would live *en famille*, as I live. Every courtesy would be extended to her as they believe hers would be extended to them. They ask an early fulfilment of this quest and an early beginning to this new position and employment.'

'And who will you nominate for this position, Mamselle?' Mrs Kent asked. 'You have met several young ladies from the village and from Cambridge. It cannot be difficult to make a choice.'

'I would like to select Emma,' replied Mamselle firmly. 'She has excellent French, a good knowledge of general subjects and, in addition, her nature fits her for this new adventure.'

'She is too young,' Mrs Kent said firmly. 'Fifteen! She is too young to travel abroad and take up a position!'

'Emma is self-reliant and resourceful,' Mamselle replied. 'Mature for her years. And her stay abroad will add to her knowledge, and give her greater confidence and poise.'

'Emma has these qualities already, Mamselle,' Emma's father, the professor, ventured dryly. 'But I agree with my wife. I cannot accept or agree to this venture. France is on the verge of a revolution. There is chaos. Their parliamentary system has broken down. Who knows what may follow this lack of discipline and control.'

'Professor,' Mamselle addressed him. 'The Count and Countess Duval would not have suggested a guest in their household had conditions been adverse, and not entirely safe. The disturbances you mention, sir, I believe are confined to the suburbs of Paris only. The Château Duval is situated in a rural area, many miles from Paris. I assure you that the château and our lives will be safe. I give you my personal pledge upon this.'

'Could someone listen to me!' cried Emma. 'I am not an inanimate object, a parcel to be discussed and passed around. I have my own will, my own point of view! I would like to go to France with Mamselle. That is my wish, my desire, and what I truly long to do. Father, please allow me this. Please!' Emma ran to her father and took his arm. He turned his face to her with an expression of caring and love. He smoothed her hair. He kissed her on the forehead and he spoke to Mrs Kent.

★ ★ ★

Mamselle and Emma left for France at the end of the week. To her surprise, Mrs Kent wept a little at Emma's departure. Her father embraced her and gave her an ample present of money in a leather draw-purse.

This Emma placed in the pocket of her cloak. It was her armoury for the future. As the coach arrived, a weak sun came out and gilded everything with a spring-like radiance. It seemed to Emma a good omen of what was to come and she welcomed the future without hesitation or reserve.

She was off to France where Armand lived. She did not know where he was or how she could contact him, or whether they would meet again. But all prospects looked good. And she would welcome what would take place with courage, expectancy and a good heart.

She waved goodbye, and set her face towards France. A vista which would change her life.

2

Emma and Mamselle caught the boat at Dover for their voyage to France. Mamselle now asked Emma to call her Yvette and not address her as Mamselle.

'We are companions now, Emma. Equals. There is no difference between us now. Come, let us inspect our cabin and then go up on deck.'

The sea was choppy, snapping at the ship with icy waves. Emma was glad to find she was a good sailor, but poor Yvette went pale and had to clutch the ship's rail.

The second officer of the packet came to talk to them. He seemed greatly taken with Yvette which was the usual effect she had upon unattached men.

'The unrest in France continues,' he told them, 'though the President of the Assembly and the Deputies are trying to find a peaceful solution to the country's ills. These pestilential wars have drained away the country's reserves. I trust a way may be found forward without revolution.'

'Revolution!' cried Yvette. 'What sort of

talk is this? There will be no revolution. France is too stable, too sophisticated to succumb to any such upheaval! There is unrest in Brittany, I grant you that. But it is of no moment. It will not reach Paris itself. Paris is the keystone of France. That great city will brook no insolence from the peasants of Brittany!'

'Yet there is talk that the Bastille will be stormed by insurgents, Miss Yvette,' replied the crewman. 'And believe me, if the Bastille falls, all of France falls. The Bastille is the historic monument of France, so to destroy the Bastille would be to put a light under the timber of revolution.'

The officer moved away with a salute to them both. Without further word they went below.

In the cabin Emma pondered what had been said. It seemed that the situation in France was more advanced, more threatening than they had known in England. She remembered her father's words and a frisson of apprehension ran through her. But there was nothing she could do now. Only face events and make the best of them as they confronted her.

There was a carriage waiting for them

on the quay at Boulogne, and so they began their journey through the French countryside. Emma thought there was a great deal of traffic on the roads: carts, barrows, people trudging along as if they were refugees, carrying their goods on their backs.

Many farmsteads stood empty and, as they drove past, fists were shaken at them and stones thudded against the sides of the vehicle.

'Cochons!' cried Yvette. 'They do not know what is good for them. They do not appreciate what they have. They are led astray by slogans, promises and bribes!'

Emma did not reply. She thought that Yvette was upset because the peaceful picture of France she had believed in previously was vanishing before her eyes.

After a long journey they reached at last the hamlet in which the Château Duval was situated. It was calm here, Emma noticed. The clamour of the roads had gone. Yvette's spirits clearly rose now and she chattered gaily as the carriage turned into the big iron gates. Emma's previous doubts lifted also, as she saw the view before her.

The château was not large but it was

beautifully proportioned. It was built of white stone with turrets and diamond-paned windows. Farmlands surrounded the whole and there were gardens laid out with trees and shrubs and a summerhouse. The setting sun seemed to coat the whole with radiance.

The Countess Duval was waiting to receive them in the panelled front hall.

Emma saw a tall woman dressed in a rather classical style. She had a healthy glow and beautiful blonde hair mounted high upon her head. Jewels gleamed on her fingers and around her throat. Her eyes were bright and her voice pleasant as she spoke.

'Welcome back, dear Yvette. And Miss Emma, welcome to our château also. Hélène, please take the valises of the two ladies to their rooms. We will all talk later. The evening dinner will be served within an hour.'

But before anyone could move, a door to the side of the hall opened and a small boy of about eight years old joined the gathering.

Emma saw a look of pride and pleasure light up the countess's face. 'This is my son, Henri, Miss Emma,' she said, and the little boy advanced to take Emma's hand. He was formally dressed in a blue velvet suit with a white lace collar. His face was rather pale, his dark eyes bright and intelligent. He bowed over Emma's hand and uttered the formal words of greeting. Then he said: 'Is it true, that in England, if a wife displeases her husband he has her head chopped off?'

'That is not usual at all, Henri,' Emma answered.

'Yet your King Henry did this, several times.'

'Perhaps kings are a law unto themselves,'

Emma answered. 'Thank you for your interest in my country's history.'

Somehow, this question and answer seemed to please everyone present. The ice had been broken in a natural way. There was a murmur of approval as Emma followed Hélène upstairs to her room. Henri waved to her from below.

★ ★ ★

Emma's room was large and commodious, furnished in mahogany in the European style. Yvette had told her that they all changed for dinner so Emma put on a dress she had brought with her of sprigged cambric with a drawstring bodice trimmed with braid. She brushed her long auburn hair which she wore loose and unconfined in the English way. She wished her freckles were not so pronounced, but perhaps they would fade in time.

At the foot of the stairs she met the countess who presented her husband, Count Maurice Duval. Emma curtsied as she had been taught and uttered the pleasantries of an introduction.

Emma noticed that the count was a stockily built man of about fifty with a clear complexion and iron grey hair. He was courteous but formal and Emma gained the impression that he was a man of competence with many interests and involved in many concerns. He escorted Emma into the dining-room.

Emma was unprepared for the magnificence of this room and the meal which followed. Chandeliers hung from the ceiling, casting myriads of crystal lights over the table and the display of viands.

The silk-covered walls seemed to reflect back the splendour of the scene. Poultry, pies, choice vegetables, creams, desserts and wines were all arrayed. The family sat down and waited to be served.

Emma ate very little. She could not help but remember the streams of peasants trudging along the highways, clearly hungry and dispossessed, facing a future they could not even envisage. There was obviously great inequality in France at the present time, she mused. Trouble was on the horizon. Indeed, it appeared to have arrived already.

At the end of the meal both Emma and Yvette were deathly tired and they asked to be excused. Emma was glad to escape the heat and fumes of the dining-room and welcomed the solitude of her own room.

It was during the night, well past midnight, Emma judged, that she was awakened by the sound of voices. She got out of bed, drew back the curtains and looked out of the window. Shadowy figures were moving around the outskirts of the château. There were no flares but in the light of the moon Emma saw the figures of workmen, beggars even. Some appeared to be footpads.

They seemed to be measuring up the exterior of the building, studying the windows and doors. Some drank from bottles and relieved themselves in the bushes. Their voices, in whispers, scarcely penetrated the air.

Were the staff apprehending poachers? Emma wondered. Suddenly the scene outside seemed like a mirage, a dream, a figment of her imagination. Emma returned to bed and fell asleep.

The next morning the countess called Emma into the salon, another large room which over-looked the front gardens.

'Dear Emma, I wish you to assist me with my study of English literature. Here is a volume of John Donne's poetry. Please help me to understand it so that I may recite it well. And later, will you take Henri for a country walk and begin his lessons in the English tongue? Yvette and I will have other matters to engage us then.'

And so life settled into a gentle rhythm at the château. Culture was the main interest and occupation of the family. The countess painted, did embroidery, or played the spinet. It was an idyllic existence. Yet Emma could not rid herself of the memory of the shadowy figures in the night who had patrolled and examined the château for their own ends.

A music master came every week to give the countess music lessons. He was an Italian whose home was in Rome. His name was Carlo Berlioz and he was a tall, handsome man with an olive skin, dark eyes and black hair curling on to his shoulders. He brought grave news from Paris where the king and queen had been under house arrest for some time.

'The Dauphin has passed away. The little boy of twelve had been ill for some time but his death has shocked everyone at the court. Queen Marie Antoinette is distraught, and King Louis, also. Some fear the queen's mind may be deranged. It will surely be a long time before the royal couple recover from their loss.'

He paused, and then resumed in sombre tones. 'I must also tell you that the Bastille has fallen. This ancient prison of France was recently attacked and overrun by revolutionaries. These disaffected persons are bent upon destroying France's heritage, before they build some new constitution more advantageous to themselves.'

'Stuff and nonsense!' cried the countess.

24

'You are speaking like a political tract! Perhaps it is a good thing that this prison has been opened up and destroyed. It was a place notorious for cruelty and persecution. People vanished there, never to be seen again. And madmen! They were incarcerated there. And debtors. Perhaps it is as well that these people were given their freedom and the blot of injustice removed.'

'It will mean more criminals upon the streets of Paris, dear Countess,' Carlo replied. 'And there are enough of those along the boulevards already. Law is breaking down, order vanishing. You would not dare to walk alone for you might be attacked. It is a sorry state of affairs in a city as elegant and beautiful as Paris.'

At the mention of the fall of the Bastille, a tremor of apprehension had shaken Emma. She remembered the words of the crewman on the boat coming over from England. She recalled, also, the destitute refugees and the watchful group of men who had surrounded the château, carefully measuring it.

Just then Yvette and Henri entered the room, for Henri also had a period of instruction from Carlo. Emma saw Yvette's eyes shine as she regarded Carlo. It was clear that the Italian musician was greatly to her liking and taste.

At the end of the session, Emma heard the countess speak to her husband.

'I wish to give a musical concert, Maurice. Or a ball. Or a fête. I love to entertain and we have not invited our friends for so long.'

'Please put that out of your mind,' the count replied. 'There must be no display, no ostentation. They are watching, these people, these social thieves. Any show of culture, anything they consider bourgeois, they will quell and destroy.

'I do not like the present atmosphere in France. The unrest in Paris is spreading to the rural districts. We must be on our guard and tell our family and guests to be the same.'

Again Emma felt both fear and foreboding. Events in Paris seemed to be moving with terrifying speed, yet life at the château seemed safe and secure. But one thing troubled Emma greatly. This was the matter of Armand. She must get in touch with him. Somehow she must let him know that she was in France and breach the circumstances which divided them.

She knew that Carlo Berlioz had many contacts in Paris. He moved between foreign embassies and in the salons of members of the court. He was an accomplished musician in his own right and was sought after for his gifts and social charms. Emma confided in him of her friendship with Armand and that she missed him constantly and wished to be in touch with him again.

'And what is the name of this gentleman, Emma?'

'I know him only as Armand. He is a cadet at the Royal Military Academy in Paris.'

'This Academy is one of the élite military corps, one of the bodyguards of the king. The barracks are at Boissy-Nord, just outside the city. I imagine there are very few cadets accepted into this unit. If you will write your letter and address it only to Armand, I will personally see that it is delivered to the Academy.'

Emma thanked Carlo and went to write her letter.

True to his word Carlo delivered the letter and the reply came back very soon.

Dearest Emma,

How pleased and surprised I was to receive your letter and to know that you are in France! I will journey to the Château Duval to see you as soon as I can. But the hours of duty here are very long, the discipline harsh and severe. But somehow I will find a way to visit.

I send warmest thoughts and sincere felicitations.

Armand.

Emma was delighted with his letter, and the fact that she was now in direct contact with Armand. She took the letter upstairs and hid it in her valise.

Her heart was filled with joy and anticipation that soon she and Armand would be reunited, a prospect which must surely have only the happiest outcome, a meeting which would bring joy to them both. Conditions in France might be grave but there was personal pleasure to come.

3

Often from the windows of the château Emma observed a man walking about and sometimes working on the boundary of the estate.

He was tall and rangily built with long dark hair and a tanned face. He wore the garb of a workman but tied a handkerchief emblazoned with the tricolour around his throat.

But it was not his working clothes which focused Emma's attention upon him, it was his attitude towards the grounds and the house.

He moved around with assurance and, more than that, he had an almost propietorial air. He looked about him as if *he* were the owner and not the count. His attitude was that the château was already his.

Emma found this deeply disturbing and approached Hélène, the housekeeper, to ask who this man might be.

'His name is Vincent Giraud,' Hélène said. 'He is a metal-worker, from Paris.

The count is employing him to repair some of the machinery on the farms. He mends the perimeter fence also.

'He comes to the kitchen door for hot water, but in an insolent way. I do not know why the count employs him. If I were in charge I would dismiss him without delay. I think he has his own purposes here. He serves no one but himself. I do not trust him and think he will bring disaster to us all.'

★ ★ ★

Each afternoon, Emma and Henri took a walk together and she gave him easy instruction in English and they talked of general subjects.

He was a delightful and companionable little boy with perception beyond his years. Emma was greatly attached to him and he gave her his boyish trust and friendship.

They walked this afternoon near a coppice which led to the nearby woods. It was there they encountered Vincent Giraud.

'So, it is the English teacher!' he cried. 'The young lady from Albion who is improving the diction of the whole family!

You are not without your attractions, Miss, I grant you that. You are not classically beautiful but you have appeal. And your hair! You wear it loose and long and not coiffured! I could run my hands through that thicket and catch rabbits in it and kill them with my bare hands!'

Emma stared aghast at this impudent and offensive statement. 'You will not have that opportunity, sir,' she said. 'Not now, or ever.'

'We shall see. You are young but time will amend that. And there are more prizes in the revolution than loot and gold. Remember that.'

Giraud now turned his attention to Henri. 'And this is the son and heir. How are you, my little man? I could teach you a few tricks, given time. And time is what I have.'

He put out his hand as if to touch Henri's head, but Henri cried, 'Do not touch me, sir. Keep away. Do not come near.' And Henri tugged at Emma's arm to pull her away.

But Giraud barred their way. 'Do not turn against me, Emma!' he cried. 'Do not repel me. You should join force with me and my compatriots. You are an employee, also. A teacher. Your cause is ours. We may be the underdogs now, but we shall triumph in the end!'

'Do your beliefs give you licence to offend a young woman and frighten a small boy?' asked Emma. 'Pardon us, please.' Emma drew Henri aside and they went on their course.

They walked on towards the summer-house and the wood.

'He desires you,' Henri told Emma.

'I know.'

'But you do not desire him.'

'Certainly not.'

'You made that plain. But he will try again to reach you, Emma,' Henri said. 'He is aggressive and determined. He wishes you ill, not well.'

They reached the summerhouse and went in and sat down. Emma had brought some sweetmeats for them and some candied fruits.

Henri took Emma's hand. 'I love you, Emma,' he said. 'When I am grown up, will you marry me? I shall be a lawyer and pass all my exams. We will have a house in Paris and a villa near Marseilles. I will be a good husband to you, Emma, and provide for you well. You are my heart's desire and

I will always love you truly.'

Emma felt immeasurably touched by the small boy's offer of devotion. She looked down into his trusting face and his bright eyes.

'But you have all your life before you, Henri,' Emma replied. 'We will consider everything when you are a grown man.'

But Emma was suddenly filled with foreboding and apprehension concerning the future for the small boy and, indeed, for them all.

For she knew that Vincent Giraud was the man she had seen from her bedroom window, leading unknown followers around the house, measuring up and taking stock of everything.

Her thoughts were serious as she went indoors.

Emma felt she must tell the count of her suspicions concerning the loyalty and intentions of Vincent Giraud. But the count was absent on business and the countess was interested only in domestic and personal affairs.

Emma wondered why the count, who was so enlightened about the political situation in Paris and in the whole of France, should be so blind as not to suspect a man in his own employment. He seemed to see no danger in Vincent Giraud; indeed, he seemed scarcely to know he was there. To him, Giraud was only a metal-worker from Paris, bent upon doing the necessary repairs to the farms and the boundary fence.

Emma pondered, also, the words of Hélène, the housekeeper, when they had been together in the kitchen.

'Why do you not leave here, Miss Emma, and return to England? You could go now while the roads are clear, before it is too late. Once the insurgents spread out from Paris to meet the malcontent farmworkers from the south, the roads will be blocked and travel impossible.'

Emma knew there was truth in those words and, indeed, she could have left the château tomorrow had she wished.

She had no definite terms of employment and she had the money her father had given her intact. She could surely have found a conveyance to take her to a channel port and from there to England and her home.

She admitted to herself that she was often homesick. She longed to see her father again and the Bell House, and the pleasant village and surrounding country-side.

And there was peace there, also. The peace of rural England, a treasure indeed! But she knew she would not go. Invisible bonds seemed to tie her to the château and to France. She felt her future was here. Her destiny, also. Not only because of the dear friends she had made at the château, but also, she knew, because of Armand. She could not leave France without seeing him again, and although she could not explain it, she felt that she was here for an indefinable purpose, something not yet revealed. Some fate she must work towards to fulfil.

★　★　★

'He is so charming!' Yvette confided to Emma. 'Carlo is polished, yet he is a man of affairs, too. And he is kind. We have so much in common. He has brought happiness and purpose to my life. I have never had a serious man friend until now. And his presence in my life has brought me only joy and content.'

Emma was pleased for Yvette, for she had noticed a growing rapport between

Carlo and her friend whenever the music master visited the château.

Allowed by the countess, Yvette turned the pages of his musical manuscripts, served him with refreshments and walked with him to the door when he departed.

Emma saw a tender kiss take place between them both. She felt sincerely glad that happiness had come to her friend.

Happiness seemed in short supply at the present time, so every occasion of it was a blessing.

★ ★ ★

On Tuesday the 4th August 1789, the National Assembly of France was called into session and the proceedings took many hours.

Proclamations were discussed and measures passed. Restrictions on pigeons and dovecotes were warmly applauded, as was the abolition of tithes.

The Rights of Man were discussed and given theoretical approval. It was agreed that these new measures must be presented to his Majesty King Louis XVI.

Count Duval was in Paris during this time and, when he arrived home he cried,

'They have dismantled the entire structure of the French social system. They have left nothing. They have been like house-breakers with hammers, smashing up a noble structure. What is now to become of France?

'The harvest in France is plentiful, indeed ample.' continued the count. 'But there is scarcely any bread in Paris. There are food riots and scenes of violence to obtain even the smallest supplies. Ordinary citizens do not know where to turn.'

It was after this that the servants began to leave the château and the workers on the farms also disappeared.

'Of course they are deserting,' Hélène told Emma. 'The commundards regard servants as equal to their masters in crime and extravagance. What they deal out to the masters, they deal out to the underlings. I am alone in the kitchen now. Miss, do you realize that? Madame does not seem to understand the situation and what I am doing.'

Emma saw that Hélène was baking vast quantities of bread, pies and cakes. She seemed to be preparing for a siege. A disquieting thought for the whole family.

Hélène again pressed Emma to return

to England. 'France's fight is not yours, Miss. Surely there is a way for you to escape before it is too late?'

Emma tried to pacify Hélène. She pondered her advice and Vincent Giraud's words. She knew, for she had seen with her own eyes, the reality of the difference between the peoples of France. But was revolution the way to solve those ills? Was violence the way forward for the French people? There was revolution in America. Was revolution catching like some plague or childhood ailment?

Now the countess seemed to rouse herself from her unseeing coma and she began to get to grips with the situation. The whole family now had to do the household chores around the château. Even little Henri carried dishes and attempted to do his own laundry.

Luckily, Emma was skilled in household tasks and helped to roast meats, sweep the rooms and do the dishes. But the unease prevalent in the château remained.

Carlo Berlioz came; he said it must be for the last time.

'There is severe deterioration in the situation,' he told them. 'All parliamentary measures have been in vain. They are ignored as inadequate. Violence is seen as the only way forward. The insurgents have confronted the King. They have set his authority at naught. Queen Marie Antoinette fears for her life, the lives of her family and her children.'

Everyone gave Yvette and Carlo privacy in which to say their farewells and make their arrangements for the future. All knew their future was obscure. Now they could only trust and hope.

The whole family ate in the kitchen now. There was no attempt at formality or the niceties of living. Little Henri stood on a stool to dry the dishes. He was patient and kind and Emma saw that in his eyes there were often flashes of humour.

Then everything changed when from afar they had a visitor, a visitor with serious intent whom they did not expect, a visitor who would affect all their various lives for ever.

4

Emma was looking out of the window of the front hall after she had completed her duties, when she saw in the distance a horseman approaching the château along the village path.

The horse was racing and was lathered from its exertions. The rider bent over the reins as he urged his mount forward. His cloak flew out behind him as he rode and his dark hair was lifted by the wind. Both rider and horse turned into the drive of the château, and Emma realized at once that this was Armand.

Armand! Armand had come to the Château Duval as he had promised he would. And she would see him in a moment! Speak to him!

Emma ran to the front door and opened it wide. Armand secured his horse and mounted the steps to the portico of the great house.

He seized Emma's hands and kissed her swiftly. 'I will speak with you later, Emma, but for now I must see the count on a matter of urgency.'

They entered the front hall and the Duval family stared at them with amazement. It so happened that the whole family were in the hallway, having just come up from the basement kitchen after taking their midday meal.

Armand strode at once to the count, and bowed before him.

'Count Duval, here are my credentials from the colonel of my regiment. Your regiment, also, for you were formerly an aide to the colonel and his staff. The colonel, wishing to show his appreciation of your friendship, has sent me with information upon which he begs you to act. There is serious looting and wrecking in Paris and he has heard that the insurgents are heading this way, towards your village and the Château Duval.

'These men spare nothing and nobody. Many are brigands posing as political leaders and hoodwinking the people. They destroy for destruction's sake — no property is sacred. Life to them is as cheap as dust.'

'My dear Armand!' cried the count. 'How can I thank you for making this journey? And the colonel. I am indebted to him. But what does the colonel propose that I do? Of course,' the count added, 'we will defend the château and our possessions with our lives!'

'No, sir,' answered Armand. 'The colonel urges you to leave here at once. To put up no defence. To quit the Château Duval and make your escape. You are no match for these men, sir. Your colonel commands you to depart and you must obey.'

The whole family stood still in the hall — still as statues as they listened to this exchange. Emma saw the countess draw Henri to her side. She glanced wildly around the foyer, contemplating her departure from the treasures of her home.

But Armand was continuing. 'You have a property in Provence, sir, but you cannot proceed there. The peasants have joined the revolution in Brittany, Provence and Languedoc.'

'It seems there is no place to go.'

'But I understand, Count, that you have a hunting lodge in the hills above Rouen. Can you not make your way there and take your family? It is primitive, I believe, but it will serve your purpose at the present time.'

Armand now crossed the hall to stand beside Emma. 'And Emma, sir, I request earnestly that you take Emma with you and secure her safety from harm.'

'But of course I will do that,' the count cried. 'I will protect Emma as if she were my own daughter. You need have no fears about that.

'But take wine, my dear Armand. Let me offer you my hospitality. It is a long ride back to Paris. Can you not stay a while and rest?'

'No, sir. I regret that I must return to the regiment at once. I have fulfilled my mission. That is all the rest I seek. I will take refreshment and water my horse later.'

Armand now held Emma's hands and kissed her cheek lightly. 'Go with the count, Emma,' Armand told her. 'That is my wish. I rely upon you to do that. I will see you again. And soon. I promise you truly. I will come to Rouen. Somehow we will be together again.'

All the family went to the front door to see Armand depart. His horse raced away again and Armand's cloak few out behind him, his dark hair curled and was lifted by the wind.

At once there was concentration in the hallway of the château. That all were to decamp now, and leave the building, was clear. But there seemed a great deal to do.

What to pack; what to take; how to proceed to the hunting lodge? Who to tell; when to return; who to trust; what to leave behind? What was vital and what was not so vital? What could the family manage without? What must be preserved? And would the Duvals ever see their beloved home again?

'Emma, will you pack for Henri, please, and yourself. And Maurice, will you require your medals and your hunting suit?' the countess asked. 'Shall I need an evening dress?' she cried. 'Shall I pack my collection of fans, my volumes of verse and my sheets of music?'

'Take only the necessities, Gabrielle,' the count told his wife. 'And hurry. There is little time. Cadet Armand impressed upon us that time is short and we must be away without a moment's delay.'

But somehow, progress was slow. Cases were packed and unpacked. The countess seemed to stand around in a daze.

Emma had little to pack and Henri helped her. He also carried his own small

44

garments to her and laid them in the valise. Emma thought that he seemed to be the only member of the family who properly grasped the situation.

They all went to bed that night with the château in chaos. Emma got up early and tried to make progress. She longed for a practical, helping hand. She missed Yvette greatly. Yvette had been given leave of absence from the château for a few days to visit a relation nearby on a family matter. Where was she? There had been no time to reach her but her presence would have been of assistance to them all.

At last they all assembled in the hall to begin the journey to safety and the hunting lodge.

They were surrounded by cases and boxes, for the countess had been unable to resist taking her extensive wardrobe. She wore her jewellery concealed about her person. She wore only a gold chain with a cross around her neck, and plain combs in her hair.

The count had been able to persuade a neighbouring farmer to allow him to hire a carriage to take them on the beginning of their journey. Emma thought she heard the wheels of the vehicle far off.

But the sound was of more than one carriage, she realized. The noise was louder, more prolonged, more intrusive. She went to the window of the foyer and looked out at the parklands outside.

A convoy of horses with riders and vehicles drawn behind them was approaching the château. They turned into the driveway in a flurry of dust and stones.

They approached the house with purpose, and a kind of confidence and authority. They were no social visitors, though, no family friends. They clearly had another agenda, both dire and malevolent. They were the communards intent upon their prey.

By this time the whole family were alerted to the arrival of the newcomers and their purpose. The count braced himself and stood at the head of the household group. He had no weapons but he was clearly prepared to defend those nearest to him with his life.

At once the front door of the château was broken down. The onslaught shattered the locks and bolts and the door itself was tossed aside. A large body of men now entered the château and took possession of the hallway.

They stood facing the Duvals with knives, rifles, pikes and other weapons. They cried slogans, threats, oaths and slanderous accusations. Their aspect was menacing in the extreme.

There were about twenty of these men, wearing a variety of clothing. But all wore a kerchief around their necks bearing the tricolour of National France. Some wore hats with the blue and white cockade. They were attempting, by their attire, to carry the authority of the French nation.

The group now parted and their leader came forward and advanced to confront the count.

Emma was not surprised to see that this man, the leader of the insurgents, was Vincent Giraud.

That this was a moment of supreme triumph for Vincent Giraud was at once clear to Emma. His eyes shone. A smile lifted his lips. He stood before the count, legs apart, a picture of arrogance and self assurance. He gestured with his hand at the foyer, its contents, and the contents of the rooms leading off this central area. When he spoke his voice was loud and harsh. It was heard by all.

'My compatriots and I represent the

National Assembly, the Jacobin Movement and the Council of Liberty based upon the Rights of Man. We are the Fourth Commune of the Paris Revolutionary Forces. We have the legal right of the New France to pursue our course. And you obstruct us at your peril.'

'What nonsense is this?' cried the count. 'I have never heard such utter rubbish in all my life! And how dare you enter my premises and wreak destruction upon my home! Begone at once. Quit the château. You have no business, legal or otherwise, here!'

'We have important business,' Vincent Giraud replied. 'And our actions have the permission of the highest authority in France. Indeed, our actions are being repeated throughout France. We are clearing away prejudice and entrenched positions. A new era is beginning. You will thank us in time.'

'Do you realize to whom you are speaking?' cried the count. 'I am Maurice Duval and my family have lived here for generations. We have fought for France in her wars. We have farmed the lands. We have contributed liberally to taxes and charities. We are the champions of the

French nation, not yourselves!'

'There will be no titles in the New France,' Giraud told the count. 'No land held by privileged families. No personal wealth to excess. All will work for the common good and all will prosper. The Bill of the Rights of Man has already been passed.'

'But not your interpretation of it!' cried the count. 'It is not a licence for theft and personal greed!'

There was now a strong murmur from the insurgents behind Vincent Giraud. Cries of disgust and impatience rose on the air. Emma saw that a more threatening stance had been taken up by the communards. They wished for action at once.

Giraud acted immediately. 'I am empowered to demand that you hand over the deeds of your properties, the accounting of your wealth and the goods of your family. There is no escape. There is no leniency. This must be done so that equal shares for all may be provided and secured.'

'No!' shouted the count. 'Never!'

'If you refuse our demands you and all your family will be taken prisoners and your wealth taken from you by force. Your illegal gains will be used for the benefit of the common people of France.'

And now the countess seemed to come alive. She raised her voice in anger, defying the invaders. 'How dare you enter our home and make these demands! We will not yield to you. We will not surrender.'

'Very well,' said Vincent Giraud, and Emma saw that this was the moment he had been waiting for. This was the moment of his triumph and his ambition's fulfilment. This was the greatest moment of his life.

'Forward!' he cried to his followers behind him. 'Take the so-called count first and then the woman and her child. Hasten. There is no time to lose. Brook no defiance. They must obey. Impose your will. The conveyances wait outside.'

What followed had, for Emma, all the clarity and confusion of a dream. The Duval family had no defences against this large body of men, armed and possessing strong determination.

There were scuffles, cries of protest, shouts of command. The members of the family were dragged forward, towards the shattered and open door.

The count hit out wildly, and the countess bit the hand of a man dragging her away from her home.

'Maman, Maman,' cried Henri as he was lifted off the ground by a stout man in a leather jerkin. And then again piteously he cried, 'Emma, Emma. Save me. Please help us!'

By this time Emma had recovered her wits and she dashed forward in an attempt to snatch Henri from the arms of his assailant. But the stout man was too much for her.

'Who is this?' he cried to Vincent Giraud. And Giraud shouted back, 'Leave her, Boussac. She is the English teacher. We have no quarrel with England. Let her go for now. I will return for her later.'

For good measure Boussac hit Emma a sharp blow across the chest, so that she fell to the floor winded and in pain. She lay on the ground unable to move.

The uproar continued around her. Somehow, Emma managed to haul herself upright and lean against a wall. The family had been dragged out of the hallway and were being pushed and lifted into one of the vehicles outside.

There were carriages lined up, an open cart like a tumbrel and a fleet of tired horses. The count was bundled into the open cart and the countess followed.

She clutched Henri close to her and laid her head upon her upturned arms. Emma saw her tears fall, like the pearls she would now never wear.

In the hallway there was chaos. Broken furniture, shattered ornaments, abandoned cases torn open. Emma staggered from the wall. She was just in time to see the convoy of carriages move away down the drive of the château and towards the open road. But she knew as long as she lived she would remember those last moments in the hallway.

Vincent Giraud put his arms around the stout man and he said, 'We have done well, Boussac. You are a trustworthy second in command. We shall rule Paris together, never fear. This château has fallen to us like a broken egg and the city of Paris will be the same.'

★ ★ ★

Emma stood alone in the ruined hall. The wind blew in from the broken door, cold and penetrating. In spite of her attempts at courage, tears now welled in Emma's eyes and fell unheeded down her cheeks. She was in a state of shock, she knew, from the fall and from witnessing the events which had overcome the Duval family, her friends and benefactors. They were almost like members of her own family to her.

She dried her eyes, trying to think what to do. It was then that she heard a distant voice and knew that she was not alone in the château.

She crossed the corridor and entered the rear area which led down to the kitchen. She pushed open the kitchen door and looked inside.

The kitchens of the château were almost like dungeons, deeply situated underneath the main house and constructed of stone walls and flagged pavings. The pots and pans and other kitchen equipment were plentiful and gleaming. There was a slow-burning stove and a central scrubbed table. And seated at this table were Hélène and Yvette, who had returned from her family in time to witness the horrific scene.

'You do not need to tell us!' cried Hélène. 'We saw and heard everything. We watched them take the family away from the rear doors. The cochons. Pigs. Villains! They will live to give account of their crimes!'

'Dear Emma,' added Yvette. 'How can you forgive me for not coming to your aid? You coped valiantly alone. But I have had an accident. I am incapacitated. Look!' And Yvette lifted her skirts and Emma saw that her ankle was red and swollen.

She sat with it propped upon a chair but it was clearly a serious sprain which had torn the muscles of her leg.

'I cannot put it to the ground. And Hélène here has to do everything for me.'

'Sit down and take coffee,' Hélène advised Emma, for Hélène believed that food and drink brought solace to many ills. 'Have a piece of this Normandy cheesecake. And dry your eyes, Petite. There was nothing any of us could do. We must leave the family to Providence. They are now beyond our aid.'

Then Yvette continued, speaking hurriedly and in a frenzied way.

'Do not think I am unfeeling or insensitive. I realize the danger to the family. But truth to tell I am overwhelmed by the turn in my own affairs at the present time. Overwhelmed and astounded. Listen to my news, Emma. And it is good news indeed! Carlo Berlioz has asked me to marry him and I have accepted. We are betrothed. This has brought great happiness to my heart. When we are married we shall live in Rome. And now I must give you further information about Carlo. This is something you must know.'

Yvette paused and then resumed. 'Carlo was not only a music master in Paris, he was also a trusted employee of the Italian Government. He was an envoy for them. He could move freely about the great houses of Paris and he gained much information of use to his masters in Rome.'

'He was a spy!' Emma said.

'He preferred to be called an envoy,' Yvette told her, 'but that is by the way. He was apprehended in the course of his work. The National Assembly were outraged that a foreign country, Italy, should scrutinize their constitution and the events of the recent crisis. He was ordered to leave at once and was lucky to return to Italy with his life.'

Yvette paused again and a spasm of

pain shook her frame. Hélène came to her aid and gently bathed the inflamed and swollen area of her limb.

Yvette resumed. 'But during his final days in Paris he had been instructed to hand a package to a personage close to King Louis, for delivery into the king's own hand. This is a personal message from one king to another and is of considerable importance to both monarchs.

'When Carlo was forced to flee the country, he turned to me, his betrothed, and deputed me to carry out this assignment in his place. He had no option. There was no one else available. But you will see, Emma, I am unable to do this. I cannot walk across this room, let alone proceed to Paris. Therefore I appeal to you. Emma, you must take my place. You must do what I was deputed to do. Instead of my going to Paris, you must go in my stead. I beg of you, I instruct you, I charge and implore you to do this!'

Emma rose to her feet and faced Yvette aghast.

'No, Yvette,' she cried. 'I cannot do it!'

All Emma wanted now was to return

home. To return to England and the Bell House in Little Marlowe and see her father again.

She longed to quit the scene where she had endured and, indeed, suffered so much.

'Do not ask this of me, Yvette,' Emma cried again. 'I am sorry to disappoint you but I cannot do what you request.'

Yvette continued as if she had not heard. 'The gentleman you will rendezvous with in Paris is called the Duke of Rémy. This personage is a Gentleman Usher to the king and has access to him at all times. That is why he is targeted for this mission.'

'But I cannot undertake any mission for a foreign government,' Emma answered. 'I am English. I can take no part in these political matters. Surely you see my point of view, Yvette. It is impossible for me. I cannot do it.'

'I understand your scruples,' Yvette replied. 'But let me assure you that this mission is of benefit to the King of France and not otherwise. I would not ask you to undertake anything of dubious intent. Surely you know me better than that, my dear.'

Yvette drew Emma closely to her. 'I have loved you as a sister, Emma. You have brought only happiness into my life. I would not ask this of you were it not important, indeed, vital to the future of France.'

Yvette drew Emma close and with swift fingers she untied the ribbons which secured the bodice of Emma's dress. From her own dress she withdrew a package which she slipped inside Emma's own bodice.

'There,' she said. 'It is beneath your heart. Guard it as you would your own heart. For it is equally valuable to yourself and to France.'

'Look, take this basket,' Yvette resumed, 'and carry it always. A lady never carries a basket but working women always transport their belongings so.

'And wear this cloak.'

There was a large cloak with a hood of dark material which belonged to Hélène on a chair nearby. 'Keep the hood over your face. Walk quietly. Be circumspect. Attract no attention. You must walk to the village of Aix-de-Rhône, which is about ten kilometres from here. This is a junction for staging coaches. You will easily find a place on a coach going to Paris.'

'But Yvette,' Emma cried. 'Where shall I find this Usher to the King? Where does he live? What are his movements?'

'To be frank, I do not know,' answered Yvette. 'Carlo had not time to tell me. That is something you must find out for yourself. But I advise you to be off,' cried Yvette. 'You must not miss the coach to Paris. You must not loiter in these regions. Time is important. You must make haste. You have money?' she asked.

'Yes, upstairs. The money my father gave me before I left England.'

'Good. That eases the way, removes the difficulties.

'Now, we must say farewell. God speed and God bless you, my dear.'

Yvette embraced Emma and Hélène embraced her also. Watched by the two women, Emma made her way from the kitchen and mounted the stone steps to the upper hall.

She stood outside on the portico and considered the journey and her mission. She had committed herself to this errand because there had been no other way. And she felt an inner conviction that this was now, finally, something she was driven to; something she must do. Not only would she be nearer Armand, but she would be helping in some small way, and perhaps making a better future for the Duvals.

She contemplated the driveway before her, and the village path which led to Aix-de-Rhône. Then she went down the steps and began to walk the ten kilometres to the coaching station.

5

The air was pleasant this morning; a slight wind blew, ruffling the hedgerow flowers and the tall grasses on the verge of the road. Above her, Emma saw birds fly and the clouds move slowly across the arc of the sky. She moved purposefully forward.

She tried to be inconspicuous as Yvette had suggested to her. She held the cloak closely about her and kept the hood over her head. The basket was a good disguise, she decided. She also carried a small case containing her personal belongings and a change of clothing.

She was suddenly glad again that she had led an outdoor life back in England and was used to walking and preserving her strength, for she knew that a hard task lay before her. Somehow she must reach the coaching station before the last vehicle set out on its way to Paris.

Other people passed her now, or she passed them on the wide and dusty road. Refugees trudged along, their possessions on their backs. Other working men and women thronged the pathway. And coaches sped by, scattering dust and stones upon pedestrians whom they entirely disregarded.

It was inevitable that Emma's thoughts should be intense and deeply emotional. She could not rid her mind of the images of the Duval family being carried away. Their cries of defiance and the piteous call for help uttered by little Henri seemed to be with her still. She hoped that Yvette's optimistic view of the situation was correct.

She pondered also the mission upon which she was now engaged. Somehow she must find this unknown Duke of Rémy and deliver the package entrusted to her care. She touched the bodice of her dress lightly to make sure the precious letter was still safe and properly hidden. She did not want any mishap to occur to the document destined to be delivered to a king.

And then her spirits rose, for she had another reason for her journey to Paris. She had another mission to undertake when she arrived. She would see Armand!

Yes, when she had located the duke and handed over the letter, then she would go to the barracks of the Corps Royale at Boissy-Nord and request to see Cadet Armand. That she did not know his full name did not matter. He would come to see her at once, and they would be reunited. She would once again hold out her arms to him, see his smile, feel his hands take hers and their lips be enjoined in a kiss! She smiled at the vision and an elderly stonemason bowed to her and touched his cap. In her innocence, Emma didn't anticipate the difficulties that might face her. Perhaps, had she done so, she would have travelled with a heavier heart.

The traffic became more intense as she drew nearer to the coaching station. It was clear that many coachmen wished to reach Aix-de-Rhône to rest themselves and water and feed their horses before the last lap to Paris.

Travellers on foot pressed forward also. There was a mêlée on the road, a band of army deserters added to their confusion. Emma was jostled and she clung tightly to her basket. It contained fruit and some oddments of food which Hélène had pressed her to take.

It was late in the afternoon when Emma finally approached The Golden Pheasant, which was the name of the vital coaching inn before Paris. That this was the head of a busy junction was now clear.

Drivers and passengers were both entering and leaving the inn. Ostlers attended to the horses and carried luggage to and fro. Some travellers were drinking outside the inn, shouting and toasting one another.

Dust rose from the wheels of carriages as the horses were reined in, both upon arrival and for departure. And the noise! It seemed a kind of panic was raising voices and adding to the clamour.

Emma stood on the far side of the road and watched the scene. She realized that it was going to be very difficult to cross this road and reach this inn which must be her immediate destination.

She became conscious, suddenly, of a small girl who was standing close to her and who was clearly also wishing to cross the busy highway. She was aged about nine or ten and was dainty in appearance with fair hair braided around a round and pleasant face. She hopped about uncertainly as she waited for a break in the traffic. Emma saw that she was slightly lame with one leg shorter than the other.

Emma addressed her kindly. 'Would you care to take my hand, so that we can cross this road together?'

'Why, thank you,' replied the young girl. She smiled up at Emma and eagerly took her proffered hand.

'What is your name?' asked Emma, and the young girl replied, 'Babette.'

Emma thought that this suited her and said so. The small exchange seemed to please the young girl and they began to chat in a companionable way. Suddenly there was a break in the traffic and they hastened across the road together.

They were in the forecourt of the inn now, and facing the front doorway. Emma saw a man standing athwart the entrance wearing a leather apron. He was a stout man and, beneath the apron, was well-dressed. He looked about him in a supervisory way.

This was clearly the keeper of the inn. Babette ran towards this man and cried, 'Papa, Papa, this *jeune fille* assisted me across the road and gave me these!' She held aloft a bag of sweetmeats which Yvette had slipped into the basket on the kitchen table of the château. 'Look, fondants! Bonbons! Her name is Emma and she is going to Paris. May she take *déjeuner* with me, please, Papa? She is a new friend for me. I enjoy her company so much!'

The innkeeper turned to Emma. 'Thank you for your assistance to my daughter. I am Pierre Marachel, the owner of this inn and property. If you would take the midday meal with Babette, I would be gratified. This way. Please enter the inn. This way.'

Inside the inn, Emma saw there was a flurry of activity on all sides. Meals were being served, trestle tables cleared, ale was being poured, customers were in and out. The smell of cooking, ale and tobacco hung heavily in the air.

Pierre conducted them to a table set apart from the main concourse. This was clearly a private table for the innkeeper and his family.

'Pray be seated. I will send a serving man to attend to you.' And Pierre turned to go.

But Emma could not sit down. She stood immobile. She was filled with embarrassment and consternation. She could not eat or drink. She could not move. Catastrophe had overwhelmed her.

She had no money.

She remembered that she had not gone upstairs at the château, for her travelling case had been already packed and was in the hall.

The purse containing the money which Emma's father had given her in England still lay on the bedside table in her room at the château.

That she was to be a guest for luncheon with Babette was clear. But afterwards, what then? Wary though she was of confiding in a complete stranger, Emma knew she had no option but to do so.

'Please, Monsieur Marachel, stay. May I speak to you privately?' Emma told him of her predicament, that she had come directly from the château and what had occurred there.

'You have my sympathy,' the innkeeper said. 'To see the abduction of your employers and not know their fate is a grievous thing. But sympathy will not gain you a seat on a coach travelling to Paris! Hard cash is required for that.'

He then looked at Emma closely. 'But you are personable,' he said, 'of good education. And you have been kind to my daughter. Wait here and I will see what I can do.'

The serving man now brought various viands to the table and a pewter jug of coffee. Babette pressed Emma to eat and, to please her, Emma tried a portion of stew and sipped the coffee. But she could not relish the meal or the occasion. She knew her fate hung in the balance. She could only trust to good fortune and fate.

After a short time Pierre returned to their table. He spoke to Emma.

'There is a possibility of a vacant place in a private carriage journeying to Paris. This conveyance is the property of Maître Barre, an attorney well known in this area. He is travelling with his invalid son. It is a carriage with four seats and only two occupied. Maître Barre has asked to see you. Come this way, Miss Emma, please.'

Maître Barre sat alone at the central table of the inn, which showed his importance and his wealth. He had clearly had a good meal for there were many covers on the table and a choice bottle of wine.

Emma saw that the maître himself was a stockily built man of about fifty. He had a florid face with iron grey side-burns and moustache. His eyes were very penetrating and bright. He observed Emma first without saying a word. Then he bade her good day and Emma replied.

'Your cloak is that of a working woman but your dress shows another occupation,' Maître Barre began. 'Your accent is not *paysanne*. Monsieur Marachel has told me your history and I offer my commiserations. But that is not the reason for this meeting, I know. Pray be seated and hear me out.'

The maître resumed. 'I am travelling to Paris accompanied by my son, Philippe, who is indisposed. Oh, it is nothing serious. His malady is not contagious. He is not insane. He has no fever, nothing like that. But he has *ennui*. He is listless, he cannot concentrate on his studies. He seems to be in some kind of decline. The doctors are unable to help him, and I myself am at my wits' end in the matter. I have an important case to attend to at the legislature in Paris tomorrow. I must give my mind to my brief and concentrate upon my papers. I cannot give the time to attend to my son. If, therefore, Miss Emma, you would care to travel with us and minister to the small wants of my son,

I would be pleased. In that way I can work undisturbed, yet know that my son has the attention and company he requires.'

Emma accepted this offer with alacrity and sped away to tell Babette and Monsieur Marachel of the proffered invitation. She thanked both Babette and her father for their kindness and consideration to her and promised Babette that she would return to see her as soon as that was possible in the future.

She gathered up her bag and basket and went outside to join the concourse where the carriages and horses awaited. It seemed that fortune had smiled upon her and she was able to begin another part of her journey and commission.

The air seemed brighter, the traffic less intense. Emma felt she was on her way to Paris at last.

Maître Barre's carriage was a serviceable but elegant conveyance, well painted, with a coachman in livery on the driver's seat and two well-groomed horses already reined in and eager to depart.

Emma mounted the steps and entered the vehicle. And so she saw Philippe Barre for the first time.

Before her, seated in a corner of the

coach, was a young man of about nineteen years old. He had long limbs, well formed, and a countenance which took Emma's breath away.

His face was shaped on classical lines, with a straight, almost Grecian nose and curved lips. His hair was light brown and lay in tight curls around his head. He resembled the pictures of a Greek philosopher Emma had seen in a teaching manual at the Bell House. But his eyes were bright and he extended to her a well-shaped hand.

'You see before you, Miss Blythe, a broken reed, an earthenware pot shattered. Please excuse me if I do not rise. You are welcome to share our journey. Please be seated at my side.'

Emma took the proffered hand in her own. 'It is a pleasure to meet you, sir. And I am grateful for the favour of admittance to your coach.'

Maître Barre now entered the carriage and arranged himself and his documents upon the seat facing Philippe and Emma. With a word to the coachman, the vehicle drew away.

Philippe Barre now began to talk to Emma. He seemed glad of the company, eager to unburden himself of his personal thoughts.

'I am a student at the University of Paris, reading law, as my father did previously. I hope to assist my father in his legal work in due time.'

Philippe described his courses, his tutors and the essays upon which he was engaged. Emma replied, telling him of the work at Cambridge, which she had learned from her father, and describing also her own studies conducted in the library of the Bell House.

'I could do more, much more,' Philippe was concluding, 'were I not affected by this malady. It makes my work a toil and my life difficult.'

Emma sat quite still and observed Philippe. She saw the pallor of his face, his bright yet shadowed eyes, the lassitude of his frame and his drawn out speech.

She began to speak to him seriously.

'If I may address you on a personal level, sir,' she said, 'I am acquainted with your ailment and its symptoms. My own mother suffered so during the latter part of her life.'

Emma remembered the severe headaches, the days spent in a darkened room, the feeling of nausea, the longing to eat, yet the aversion to food.

'My mother also found that simple remedies were more effective than medicated draughts purchased from the apothecary. Allow me, sir.' And Emma took her own personal handcase and drew from it a phial of lavender oil which she carried with her always. She drew from it the stopper and leaned forward towards Philippe.

'A female unguent!' cried Philippe.

'Be patient, sir, and permit me,' said Emma as she drew the stopper from the phial across the forehead of Philippe and down to his temples, near to his hair-line.

At once the fragrance of the herbal flower filled the carriage. It brought with it the scent of hedgerows, of wild flowers, of grasses growing near a lake, of summer winds ruffling apple blossom, of bees amid the purple sprays of lavender.

It reminded Emma of a picnic.

A picnic! Emma opened the lip of her basket and took out some fruit and a clean napkin. 'And now a light meal,' she continued. 'To further reduce the pressure and give energy.'

Emma also realized, suddenly, that she

was herself ravenously hungry. It was many hours since she had had a meal and she had forgotten the small sips of stew she had taken at the inn.

'With your permission, sir,' she said to Maître Barre. And she added to the fruit home-made biscuits topped with chopped nuts, raisins and crystallized fruits.

At once the atmosphere of the carriage was lightened as they all joined in the impromptu meal. Maître Barre himself peeled the fruit and accepted a biscuit. Emma knew he had observed her attention to Philippe, though he had uttered no word. She sensed that he approved her actions and was pleased to see some improvement in the condition of his son.

For the natural oils had reduced the tension shown on Philippe's face and he had relished the picnic meal. He fell asleep almost at once. His breathing was deep and regular. He appeared more at ease, more composed.

The carriage sped on towards Paris and the atmosphere in the coach was quiet and self-contained. Maître Barre still scrutinized his papers and Emma sat looking out of the window of the coach as the fields, cottages and farmsteads of France all seemed to speed by in the now rapidly fading light.

Emma saw herself suddenly reflected in the window; she appeared to float on air beside the carriage. And suddenly, as if it were a dream, she saw the figure of Armand. She saw his oval face, his brown eyes, his hair which grew in curls over his head. She saw his tall frame, the ease and swiftness with which he moved; the aura he gave of directness yet compassion.

I shall see him soon! she told herself. I promise myself that. I shall see him soon!

The vision faded and Emma saw now that they were reaching the environs of Paris and that their journey would soon be at an end.

Darkness fell as they entered the city. She saw flares, buildings, throngs of people; all the business of a great metropolis. Yet she knew she had scarcely begun her search.

Maître Barre's coach took a circular route around the city to enter a western suburb. The coachman halted the horses at last in a quiet and clearly exclusive square.

Emma looked with interest at the home

of her new legal friends. She saw a large square house with a paved courtyard facing the street. Chestnut trees grew at the side of this dwelling and Emma saw, in the lamplight, tiny butterfly-like petals of blossom upon the stone flags of the path.

'Welcome to Chestnut Lodge!' cried Philippe, now fully aroused from his sleep. He sprang down from the carriage and opened the iron gate.

It was now that Maître Barre addressed Emma.

'May I ask, Miss Blythe, if you have accommodation for the night?'

'No, sir,' Emma answered. 'I have nothing arranged.'

'May I enquire also, as to your errand in Paris?'

'That is confidential, I am afraid.'

'May I venture to press you for the name of the person or establishment you are hoping to meet?'

'I do not know where this person is lodged, sir. I must begin my search tomorrow.'

'You are discreet, very discreet,' commented Maître Barre. 'An attribute I admire in my profession. But your errand is clearly not criminal or unlawful. This is

76

something I approve. I am therefore pleased to offer you the courtesy of my home for the night. I could not allow a young lady such as yourself to venture alone into Paris at the present time. You would be in danger of your life and neither Philippe nor I would care to expose you to that risk.

'Philippe! Take Miss Emma's luggage!' And to Emma herself, the Maître said, 'Please follow me into the house.'

Inside Chestnut Lodge there was a warmth of stoves burning and of enclosed space. The walls of the hallway were panelled in dark wood with several doors opening off the central area.

There were carpets upon the parquet floors and also on the treads of the stairs which led upwards.

A pleasant youngish woman now appeared and greeted the Maître and Philippe warmly yet civilly. 'This is Arlette, my housekeeper,' Maître Barre said. 'Miss Blythe is to be our guest for tonight, Arlette. Please make her welcome and attend to any wants she may have.'

Emma thanked her new host and Philippe and followed Arlette upstairs. Her room was at the rear of the house, facing yet another courtyard and further trees drooping now in the sudden chill of mist and darkness.

It was a large room, furnished as Emma's room at the château had been, with heavy pieces of dark wood furniture, and a four-poster bed. Emma looked longingly at this bed, for truth to tell, she was deathly tired. But she rallied herself, made a hasty toilet then made her way downstairs.

She had been asked to share the evening meal which was served in a panelled room at a long table. Maître Barre sat at the head of the table with Philippe and Emma at his side.

Arlette brought in a generous casserole with bread and vegetables. Later she served a fruit compôte with soured cream and sweet biscuits.

A bottle of Burgundy was brought to the table, diluted with sugar and water. Maître Barre now began to speak.

'You have come to Paris, Miss Emma, to a city divided not in two but in several, indeed, many ways. There are currents and undercurrents. Factions war with factions. Old scores are paid off and new animosities created. All believe their own philosophy and their own remedy for the ills of France. But for myself, I am neutral. I side with no party but pursue my own course, guided by my own principles and experience of life.'

He paused and Arlette poured coffee. The maître resumed. 'I am consulted by members of the government — such as it is. The clergy, the civil servants all consult me. Even the revolutionary leaders approach me, for they know the value of the force of law. I receive them all and I am impartial to all. And this is how I wish my household to remain.'

Is the maître telling me not to involve himself and Philippe in any revolutionary activity? Emma asked herself. He did not know her errand in Paris, of course, but perhaps he guessed that her mission was important and involved other people beyond herself.

'I respect your wishes, sir,' Emma told the maître pleasantly. 'And trust I shall not involve you and your family in any adverse matter in any way.'

The maître smiled and seemed pleased with Emma's response. Emma now felt quite overcome with fatigue and asked to be excused. She made her way upstairs, longing only for the comfort of the four-poster bed.

She was surprised to find that Philippe had followed her from the room and was escorting her up the stairs.

They paused at the door of her room.

It was clear that Philippe wished to speak to her seriously and Emma stood still and looked up into his face.

'Emma,' he began. 'I wish to thank you sincerely for your kindness and attentions to me in the carriage. Your ministrations have been efficacious, yes, but it is for more than that I am grateful and wish to express to you my appreciation.'

He paused. 'No one, until yourself, had considered my malady seriously and had taken the thought and time to proffer some simple and practical remedy. It is this which has touched me deeply and this which has lodged in my mind. Believe me, I shall always value your perceptions and timely efforts on my behalf.'

'But it was so little!' Emma replied, wishing to lighten the atmosphere. 'Anyone would have done the same! Think no more of it, please!'

But Philippe continued. 'There is another matter on which I wish to speak to you. To confide in you again, if you will give me leave.'

He paused. 'It concerns the circumstances of my youth. When I was a pupil at the academy, there was another student who made it his business to torment, badger and humiliate me. I gave him no cause for this but he persisted in his campaign of denigration and humiliation. I seemed to have no defence against him, for I was in poor condition at the time. It was the beginning of my nervous malady. It has been a circumstance which has haunted me all my life.'

'I regret to hear this,' Emma answered soberly. 'Perhaps time itself will heal all these wounds.'

Philippe persisted. 'If I can assist you at any time in the future, please call upon me. My best services will be yours.'

Philippe bowed over her hand and opened the bedroom door for her. Emma closed the door behind her and prepared for bed. As she lay at last in the warmth and comfort of the feather-bed, she pondered her course for tomorrow. That it would be difficult and dangerous, she did not doubt. But she had made a friend.

She felt a strong rapport between

Philippe and herself. There was a bond between them now, which she thought would endure. He was a man of integrity, who did not pledge himself lightly. She felt suddenly strengthened and encouraged.

She would face tomorrow with courage and high hopes. And with this reassurance, she fell asleep.

6

The household was up early, each person busy with their own activities. Arlette bustled about and Maître Barre prepared to leave for his legal chambers.

Breakfast was laid out informally in the dining-room. There were hot rolls and confiture and a kind of frumenty. Hot coffee was in a jug on the sideboard.

Philippe had a kind of alcove off the main saloon in which he worked and studied his papers. It was there that Emma found him, after breakfast, for she wished to speak to him seriously. She required his immediate help.

She had decided to take Philippe into her confidence. Not entirely, but in part. Philippe heard her out.

'The Duke of Rémy!' he cried. 'No, I am not acquainted with this gentleman, Emma. I do not move in high social circles such as you suggest. It is a dangerous quest to try to find this gentleman and one doomed to failure, I think. There are many aristocrats living in Paris, in hiding.

Though many have fled the city for the country or foreign parts.'

Philippe paused and looked at Emma earnestly. 'Also, for you to attempt to find this high-born man openly, will mark you as a confederate of his class and liable to arrest and persecution yourself. For the revolutionaries arrest not only the aristocrats themselves but their friends, servitors and acquaintances. I urge you on no account to begin this search, Emma. And certainly not to continue with it.'

Emma looked at Philippe steadily. 'But nevertheless, that is what I must do,' she said. 'Will you assist me, please? Do you know where this man might be? Can you help me to discover his whereabouts or his fate?'

'What is the basis of this errand you are engaged upon, Emma?' cried Philippe. 'What mission have you undertaken? Why? And for whom?'

'I cannot tell you, Philippe,' replied Emma. 'To do so would betray a confidence and betray also those who have trusted me.'

'You are obstinate, Emma,' replied Philippe. 'You have a will of your own. But let me think for a moment.' He paused, then resumed. 'I have no information whatsoever concerning the person you seek, but I believe I can direct you to someone who may give you directions. Go to the Café Tabac in Rue Poland. Ask for the proprietor, Sigi Lasard. He is a man on good terms with both sides. With both the aristocrats and the insurgents. His café is a clearing house for information and orders from all quarters.'

Philippe paused again, deep in thought. 'If he demurs, tell him that you come from the Golden Clasp.'

'The Golden Clasp!' repeated Emma. 'What is that?'

'Dear Emma, it is an association of socially-minded citizens of France who wish to see their country progress by legal and constitutional means instead of revolution, cruelty and mayhem. It is gaining ground all the time, in all quarters, but of course it is detested by the revolutionaries. So use this information sparingly, Emma, for it is a tinder bomb. As is the nature of your request.'

Philippe now moved aside the legal books and papers he had been studying, and cried, 'Allow me to come with you, Emma! I can be your guide in Paris, your champion, your right arm in all things!'

'I am sorry, but no, Philippe,' Emma replied. 'This is a journey I must make myself alone.'

She did not add that she did not wish to endanger Philippe himself. He would not wish for this caution. But she reiterated her decision. 'I must go alone and I must make a start at once.'

Emma thanked Philippe for his attention and assistance then went to the kitchen to thank Arlette for her kindly welcome. She then put on her enveloping cloak and picked up her basket.

'God go with you!' cried Philippe as he escorted her to the front door.

Emma smiled her farewell and stepped out of the environs of Chestnut Lodge to face the streets of Paris and what would await her there.

She set off with a purposeful stride, moving steadily from this western suburb towards the central areas of the city. Emma was glad of her cloak and basket. She felt that these had served her well before and would again act as a covering disguise.

But as she progressed towards the inner reaches of this famous and beautiful city, her steps slowed and a kind of consternation and dismay filled her.

For everywhere it seemed that the elegance of this city had been defaced and the glories of its architecture and monuments had been brought low.

She saw that many of the prestigious houses she passed had their windows broken and the shops were empty and boarded up. The parks were neglected and overgrown. On the pavement rubbish piled up and the gutter ran with filthy water. Rats ran freely in basements and through the litter. Groups of ragged and abandoned children ran through the streets in gangs, their cries disturbing the pigeons, floating high on the tainted air.

No one seemed to be working. Men lounged about the streets or assembled at street corners. Women, also, sat in doorways and alleys without occupation but clearly in defiance or distress.

Emma tried to shut out her reactions to these scenes. She knew she would never forget them; for now she felt she could not afford the luxury of openly expressed sorrow and regret.

She found at last the Rue Poland and located the Café Tabac. It was a poor place, she thought, and it clearly had few customers this morning.

She opened the door and went inside.

The café was empty, and Emma softly called the name of the proprietor. A curtain parted and the gentleman she sought stood before her.

Sigi Lasard was a man in his late thirties, tall and thin, with an air of reliance and experience. His shrewd eyes observed Emma closely before he spoke.

'Good morning, miss. To what do I owe your presence in my café this morning?'

'I have come to ask for information, sir. I trust you will be kind enough to give it to me.'

'I am wary about imparting information to strangers,' Sigi Lasard replied. 'May I know your name and your business, young miss?'

Emma at once identified herself as an English teacher with the family Duval at their château in the country. Sigi Lasard snorted with disbelief.

'An English teacher!' he cried. 'What an extravagance! What unnecessary expenditure! No wonder the masses turn against the aristocrats when they see such profligacy, such waste!'

Emma was nettled by his reply but before she could answer, Sigi Lasard went on. 'And here you are, a foreigner, eating the bread of France while there is not enough food to go round in Paris. Do you know that children are starving here? Old people the same. England is awash with food, but this is not the case in France, now.'

'I assure you, sir, my wants are very small,' Emma rejoined. 'And I brought food into Paris when I arrived yesterday.'

Sigi appeared mollified by this reply. 'Are you a spy, then?' he asked. 'You with your youth and innocent expression may well be an agent for Albion. Perfidious Albion!' he cried. 'England is well known on the continent for deceit and double dealing.'

Emma stood her ground before him. 'I have not come for fortune telling or defamation of my country,' she said. 'I have come with a civil request and I expect a civil answer. I have come to ask you to direct me to the whereabouts of the Duke of Rémy, a Gentleman Usher to King Louis XVI of France.'

A shadow fell over Sigi Lasard's face, and he became silent.

'It is more than my life is worth to supply you with this information,' he said soberly. 'We could both be killed. I must ask you to leave.'

But Emma did not move. Instead she stepped closer to the café owner. She lowered her voice, yet spoke with confidence and authority. Her eyes did not leave his face.

'I come from the Golden Clasp,' she said.

At once Sigi's expression changed and the whole atmosphere of the encounter was altered.

'Why did you not say so before?' he cried. 'Follow me. Come this way.'

And he drew aside the curtain and conducted Emma into the premises behind the bistro and bar.

It was a surprisingly well furnished room with a simple meal already laid on the table and coffee simmering on the hob of a stove.

'Pray be seated, miss,' Sigi told her. 'Let us take refreshment before we go further.'

Coffee was then poured and croissants, hot from the oven, produced. Emma found she was again hungry and ate with an appetite of which Sigi approved.

'There would be no difficulty in giving you the address of this gentleman in the ordinary way. But for you to seek him out now will bring you to the notice of the communards. You may well draw from them the same penalties they inflict upon all aristocrats at the present time in France.'

'I must take that risk, sir,' Emma answered. 'But I will try to be careful. And discreet.'

'Someone has taught you well,' he mused. 'Young as you are, I trust you and will give you my confidence.

'The address of the duke is a large house called the Pavilion. It is situated in a central area, close to the House of Deputies. This is where many notables and officials reside.' He paused again. 'But I doubt that you will find him there. The duke is now in the hands of the revolutionaries. He has been captured and taken their prisoner. I do not know where he is. Or what is his fate.'

'Yet I feel I must start my search for him at the address of his home,' Emma replied. Some instinct told her that that was where she must begin. She did not doubt this instinct and her belief.

It was then, through the rear curtained window of the café, that Emma saw the building outside. It was a large structure at the rear of the premises and seemed to be a stockroom. Yet it was clearly something more. Emma saw the windows, the closed stout door. The place had an air of secrecy and security.

Sigi saw Emma's questioning glance. He replied to her, 'It is a hostel. My own responsibility. It is reserved for those who need it during the revolution. Some serve and have nowhere to go. They can find protection here.'

'Members of the Golden Clasp?'

'Yes, exactly,' Sigi replied.

'How do the members operate?'

'Rescue, alleviation and preparation for the eventual return to law and order in France. Their influence is widespread, though hidden at the present time. But to be a member is dangerous. Do not reveal your knowledge. Keep your information hidden and yourself safe.'

Then he changed the subject at once. 'Take every care.' He placed within Emma's basket a bag of croissants and a small pat of butter. Emma knew that this was a sacrifice and a compliment indeed.

'I visited England once,' Sigi said. 'My ship put into Portsmouth. Or was it Southampton? No matter. I grew to respect the English. I apologize for my earlier uncivil remarks.'

Emma bowed her head to accept the apology. 'Perhaps if you could visit me again, we could converse together in the English tongue,' Sigi said. 'For I am anxious to increase my proficiency in your language.'

'I shall be pleased to do so, sir,' Emma answered.

And so they parted on good terms and Emma went on her way.

She became suddenly unaccountably tired as she directed her steps towards the Parliamentary areas of the city.

She thought longingly of Chestnut Lodge with its comfort and sense of security. Before she had left the house that morning, Maître Barre had called her into his study. He had spoken to her seriously.

'I have thought again over the matter of your stay in Paris, Emma and, though I do not know your mission, nor how you will succeed in what you wish to do, I have decided to offer you the extended hospitality of my home. Please regard

Chestnut Lodge as your base in Paris and until you leave France.'

Emma felt greatly touched by this offer on the part of the lawyer but he waved her thanks aside.

'Arlette likes you. Philippe likes you. It is a long time since a young lady graced these premises with her presence. We trust to see you for the evening meal. Then we can discuss other plans.'

He paused again. 'I have appreciated your kindness to my son, Philippe. You have shown me a way forward which I did not have before. Thank you. And I hope to see you later today.'

So I have a roof over my head while I am in Paris, Emma thought. And I am among friends whom I trust and appreciate. Suddenly she longed for Philippe to be with her. In spite of his disability, he was practical and stalwart. She felt she had need of such a confederate at the present time.

But as soon as my mission with the Duke of Rémy is over, Emma told herself, I must seek out Armand. I must go without delay to the barracks at Boissy-Nord and try to contact the vanished Cadet Armand.

My love, she thought. The one I truly care for. The affirmation of her commitments and feelings suddenly strengthened her. And she strode ahead with new energy and vision towards her destination.

Emma now became suddenly aware of a crowd of people pushing and thrusting themselves along the pavements and the roads. In spite of herself, she was caught up in this throng and hustled towards a communal destination where she found herself in the Place de la Concorde.

Before her was a platform upon which stood the guillotine.

She saw the wooden structure and the oblique shining blade. A prisoner was being hauled on to the platform and strapped to a board.

Emma shrank back in horror and dismay, having no desire or intention to witness an execution. But the press of people around her held her immobile. She was unable to move and her cries were drowned in the cries of others. Fear, horror, gloating, vengeance — all were expressed in the dreadful cries which assailed her.

Emma closed her eyes. She did not wish to see the blade fall. But she saw the head of the poor wretch held aloft, its hair swinging in the wind, eyes sightless and glazing. Blood now spurted from the headless body, staining the bodies and clothing of those nearest to the platform. Some gloried in this fact; others shrank back in horror. But all around the platform the crowd was overwhelmed with emotion. Tears fell, arms were clasped; some fell to the ground.

With a tremendous effort, Emma gathered her senses to her and began to push her way out of the crowd, followed by many other spectators who wished to quit the scene.

Away from the platform there were scenes of disarray. Some women fainted, some men vomited. Emma steeled herself to quell her own emotion. She sped from the scene, drawing into her lungs fresh air, shutting from her mind the sight of death and vengeance. She knew she would never forget what she had seen. The memory of this would be for ever in her mind.

It was now, as Emma entered the legal and official area of Paris, that she became aware of a change in the citizens who passed her and those who seemed to occupy the offices and premises.

Emma was in an area occupied by the communards. The insurgents had taken over this area of Paris and had made it their own. They occupied the offices and the houses. They lounged about the streets, shouting, uttering bravado cries to one another and to the passers by.

The slogans of the revolution hung heavily in the air. It was as if the revolution itself drew strength and confidence from a repetition of the phrases which had at first brought about and had fuelled this uprising in France.

Emma strode ahead, as determinedly as she could. But she was filled with panic. She became deadly conscious of the package, the vital letter which had been entrusted to her by Yvette back in the Château Duval.

This document was in her charge. It was her sacred possession. It lay next to her skin, beneath her heart, laced within the bodice of her dress. And so it must remain until she reached her quarry, the Duke of Rémy. It must be handed to him and seen by no one else.

But what if she was stopped by a communard and searched as she had seen others so scrutinized? She decided she must get away from this area as quickly as possible. She must escape from this threatening atmosphere as speedily as she could.

She saw an alley-way before her which led off the main boulevard and into a distant square with a church and fountain.

She turned into this alley, which was quiet and deserted.

She heard her footsteps on the cobble-stones. She heard her breath also; it was a sigh of relief.

Then, halfway down the alley, a door at the side of the enclosure opened and a man stepped outside.

He stood before her and he smiled.

He stood with his legs apart in the attitude of arrogance and self-possession she remembered from their encounter in the gardens of the château.

He advanced towards her.

It was Vincent Giraud.

7

'So!' he cried. 'It is the young English teacher from the Château Duval! The miss who was too hoity-toity, who considered herself superior to a common man.

'But what are you doing in Paris, may I ask?' he resumed. 'Why are you here?'

'That is my business, sir, and not yours,' Emma replied.

'You are engaged upon some futile errand for the Duval family, no doubt,' Giraud continued scornfully. 'You are wasting your time and your purpose also.

'You turned up your nose at me, miss, because you knew I had worked in a factory and was of humble birth. But I assure you these considerations have been amended now!'

'Please stand aside, sir, that I may proceed,' Emma asked the man before her. Then she added, 'Your accusations against me are not true, as you well know.'

'Still the defiant one! Still showing spirit! You need a sharp lesson, miss. It seems I am the one to bestow it.'

'Stand aside. I do not wish to hear more.'

And then a rage of such proportions hit Emma that her face burned and she knew her eyes flashed. She drew herself upright and clenched her fists.

'What have you done with them?' she cried. 'You abducted them from their home, without ceremony, with a callous and cruel spirit. The Duval family had never offended you. They were blameless. They did not deserve what you and your men meted out to them. What of Henri?' Emma cried. She saw in her mind's eye the face of the small boy who had turned to her in his distress and had begged her to help him. But she had been powerless to do so.

Vincent Giraud came close to her now. She saw he wore the same garb affected by all the insurgents: the tricoloured hat, the blue patterned kerchief, the tight, almost military style trousers.

He was unshaven, but Emma guessed that this was not from preference, but to emphasize his union with the lower-based revolutionaries: the beggars, the riff-raff, the mendicants who had adopted the cries of liberty and fraternity as their own.

'Why should I tell you what has happened to this group of aristocrats?' Giraud asked her. 'You will not be civil with me. Why should I oblige you in any way?'

He paused, and looked at her thoughtfully. She saw his eyes take in every aspect of her figure and form, and panic filled her that he should see the outline of the package concealed within the bodice of her dress.

'Yet I like you,' he resumed. 'I liked you from the first, when we were both working in the château. You did not know that I observed you, but I did. I made plans for your future.'

'I do not wish to hear more,' Emma retorted. 'And I ask you again to stand aside so that I may be on my way.'

'No. You must hear me out. This matter is important. To me. And to you, also.'

He paused, then carried on. 'Before, at the château, when we removed the aristocrats, I was merely the head of the Fourth Commune of the revolutionary forces in Paris. But now that has changed. I now control the Fifth and Sixth Communes as well as the Fourth. This gives me control of this whole area of the city. The legislature, the Houses of Parliament and the house-hold properties are all accountable to me now. Not bad for a former factory worker who started in an abattoir, before becoming an engineer!'

'I assure you, these matters are of no interest to me,' Emma said with emphasis. 'I wish to depart. But firstly, I want to know the fate of my friends from the château.'

'Very well, since I wish for your regard and do not want you to oppose me, I will give you the information you desire. The Duval family are imprisoned, but are safe. They will face a revolutionary tribunal shortly, which will examine their crimes against France and the common people. If they are found guilty they must accept the penalty. But until then they are alive and well.

'But pay attention to me, you intransigent female! Listen to what I have to say. I am a single man. Unmarried. And soon I shall seek a consort to be by my side. This could well be you, if you please me and do not oppose me. You are young but time will amend that. And still, in spite of your opposition to me, I like you. You charm and affect me.'

Emma looked stricken.

'We could make a future together and share our common beliefs. For clearly you are a working woman now, with your rough cloak and heavy basket. You could live a life of luxury, for there are rich pickings from the homes of the aristocrats. Jewellery. Ornaments. Dresses of brocade. Furs from Russia. These could all be yours if you please me and align yourself to my cause.

'I do not expect you to accept at once. Of course, you must think the matter over. But there is an alehouse nearby to which we could repair and make our plans. Come, Emma, let us go together and raise our glasses to the future. These opportunities come but seldom and must be seized without delay.'

Again rage and fury gripped Emma; her emotion was of such dimensions that she could scarcely speak. She was able to address Giraud at last.

'Do not speak to me again in this offensive and immoral way. You have committed crimes for which you will pay in time. You will not go unpunished for your violence and lechery. Stand aside and let me depart. I hope never to see you again.'

'Still showing English arrogance! But I like it. And believe me, you will come round to my way of thinking in time. But now, for the moment, a kiss. A kiss to seal our conversation and our prospects for the future.'

Vincent Giraud now came close to Emma and she saw the rough skin of his face, his bloodshot eyes and the dirt upon the uniform he was wearing.

She felt his breath upon her face, smelled the odour of wine and garlic. And she fell back against the wall of the alley-way, wondering how best she could defend herself.

Vincent Giraud now put out his hand and laid it upon her shoulder. And at the touch of his flesh, anger and opposition erupted again inside Emma.

He was in proximity to the package she carried, the package she had sworn to defend with her life. And she herself, her whole being, revolted at the thought of being close to this man, a murderer and worse.

With a swift motion she opened her basket and felt inside. Yesterday, the fruit had been ripe and tender, very palatable. But now the warmth and enclosure had ripened some of the apples to a pulp. A pear, especially, was sodden with decomposition and juice.

Rapidly, Emma withdrew this over-ripe pear in her hand and raised her arm high. She brought the sodden fruit down into Vincent Giraud's face. She pushed the pulpy mass into his nostrils, his eyes, his mouth.

He gasped with surprise and dismay and fell back. Juice was now in his hair and had fallen on his tunic. He could not see. He could not speak. He was humiliated and rendered helpless. He fell back against the wall on the far side of the alleyway. But Emma did not wait to see more.

She lifted her skirts high and, seizing her basket, ran down the alley towards the square at the end. The square with the church and fountain, which represented safety to her from the man who had so grievously offended her.

The main part of the fountain in the square was hidden from the sight of anyone in the alley-way. Emma halted beside the white cascade of water, breathless and dishevelled.

She saw that this square was a quiet place, surrounded by small dwellings, with a church on the far side. It was deserted. There was no one about.

There was a stone rim around the fountain and Emma sat there for several minutes, trying to calm her emotions. She cupped her hand and drank from the water in the base of the fountain, then splashed the clear water over her face and neck. She dried herself with her clean handkerchief and sat still, feeling her senses return.

The encounter with Vincent Giraud and the trauma of seeing the execution by the guillotine had upset her more than she wished to acknowledge. But she was determined to recover from the hiatus, to face what was ahead.

Doves flew overhead; a cat came to investigate and Emma cupped her hands again to give him a drink of water. He thanked her with his brilliant eyes and gracefully stalked away.

An old lady suddenly hobbled across the square and Emma asked her the way to the Avenue Clémence. She thanked the venerable figure, stood up and was soon on her way.

That the Avenue Clémence had once been an area of affluence and elegance was now clear to Emma.

The houses were tall, detached and of classical architecture. But many were now boarded up and had fallen into disrepair. The Pavilion, the house which Emma sought, was in the middle of this row of properties. But it was clearly occupied and life was proceeding there. It was also closely guarded by communards. They stood along the frontage, fully armed and alert. It was certainly going to be no easy matter to make enquiries and venture inside.

'That's a pretty pigeon, just ready for plucking!' Emma heard one guard say to another.

'Nay, nay. She is too proletarian for me. I shall want an aristocrat when this revolution is over. Not a person in an ancient cloak and carrying a basket.'

Emma walked past the Pavilion and proceeded down the boulevard. But she knew that at every great house there was a rear area. There was an entrance for servants and other workers. Somehow, she must reach this area and see what she could find.

She turned off into a side road and walked slowly along. She stopped. For there before her was the rear entrance to the Pavilion. The back premises. The kitchens, the bath houses, the larders, the store-rooms, the wine still.

And it was unguarded.

She looked carefully around her, expecting to see guards materialize at once. She learned later that they had been removed for being drunk while on duty. But for now, their places had not been filled. Emma stepped into the small courtyard which led to the back door.

Outside this door a woman stood emptying vegetable peelings into a container. She was stout with rosy cheeks and a mop of fair hair. She had been comely once, but now she looked impoverished and worn.

A young man in his late teens stood beside her, helping her to clear the bucket of its refuse. They both watched Emma guardedly as she came closer to them.

The woman spoke first. 'And what is it you want?' she cried. 'There is nothing for you here! I know your sort. From the city centre, decked out in working clothes to hide your true identity. You have come to find what pickings you can from the disaster which has befallen this house. Be off with you. Be gone. We want no truck with minxes of your kind here.'

Emma felt extremely put out that she was so addressed. A fiery retort rose to her lips but she stayed herself.

The young man came to her aid. 'Hush, mother,' he said. 'Let the young lady speak and explain herself. We at least owe her that.'

Emma then began, in a civil and straight-forward way, to explain her presence in France. She stated that she had formerly been employed as an English teacher and companion to the family Duval and had lived at their château as a guest.

At the mention of the word Duval, the whole atmosphere changed.

'You worked there? For Count Maurice and Countess Gabrielle? But I know them. They are good people. I began my working life in the kitchens of the château. I married from there. I married the steward, François. Emile was born there, were you not, son? Don't you remember how you used to play on the lawns around the summer house and ramble in the woods? So long ago, but they were happy days. So if you would care to enter my kitchen, miss, I shall be glad to receive you.'

The kitchens of the Pavilion were extensive and very clean. But there was no sign of any cooking or food.

'I am Noelle Deschamps, the housekeeper here. And Emile is the door-keeper, waiter and general factotum. I would offer you refreshment but I have nothing to hand. I cannot buy food for we have not been paid. We were paid regularly before when the duke was in residence. But since the communards commandeered this place, they have not given us one sou. Before they took power they promised us great things. A sharing out of property. Abundance for all. Work and equal status at all times. But none of this has materialized. Instead of that, they take everything. And they are insolent and offensive to us. They treat us worse than dogs, for they despise us. Which is something the duke himself never did.'

Emma knew that she must try to calm the housekeeper down and stem this tide of injustice and state her business at the Pavilion.

'Madame Noelle, I have come to see the Duke of Rémy personally. I have important business to discuss with him. Could you direct me to him, please?'

'You have come to the right place, miss, but at the wrong time. The duke is not here. He is under house arrest in his own home, confined by the military guards of the Commune. But today he has been allowed out of the premises to attend a funeral at the cemetery of St Ignatius, near Chantilly. His personal valet, Rollo, has died. And the insurgents have allowed him to go, under close guard, to mourn his retainer.'

It was at this moment that the main door opened and a man entered the kitchen. He was tall and broadly built with a red face and bushy black hair. He looked about twenty-eight years old, Emma thought. His expression was genial and pleasant. He carried a tray aloft with one hand. Upon it, Emma saw two small loaves of bread.

'Two loaves for today! And when shall I be paid for these?' he cried. 'Oh, I know, Noelle, you, yourselves, have not been paid. Yet this situation for we tradesmen is getting serious. I cannot keep the bakery going without money. Hard cash. Not credit. I must feed myself also and my horse, Pegasus.'

He grumbled on, but in a rather weary, unthreatening way. Then he saw Emma.

'But who is this, pray? Present me, please, to your young lady visitor.'

'This is Georges Fabre, a master baker and a former national guardsman. Georges, this is Miss Emma Blythe, an English teacher, who seeks the duke upon some personal business. It is all right, Emma, you may speak freely in front of Georges — he has no love for the communards.'

Emma now began to see some gleam of light in this situation. She spoke to Georges, and said: 'Sir, I am desirous of travelling to the cemetery of St Ignatius, near to Chantilly. For Madame Noelle informs me that the duke is there, mourning a retainer, deceased. Could you direct me, please? If I know the way it will simplify matters for me. For I do not know the district at all. Indeed, I am a total stranger in Paris making my way by hearsay and enquiries.'

Georges looked at Emma doubtfully. 'Chantilly is a long way from here, the cemetery also. It will be a difficult journey for a young lady at a loss and unaccompanied. But come now, let us not lose hope. I can direct you by the shortest route, certainly. Come and sit by me at this table and I will draw a map for you. This will show you the easiest route and also where to avoid.'

He drew from his pocket a notebook and a black crayon. He pulled out two chairs and they sat down.

'Could we have coffee please, Noelle?' Georges cried.

But Noelle would have none of this.

'Why this rigmarole?' she cried. 'What a waste of time this is! There is no need for Miss Emma to go to Chantilly at all. If you cannot see the father, surely you can see the son, instead?'

Emma looked at Noelle, uncomprehendingly. 'Yes, he is here,' Noelle resumed. 'The Cadet Lieutenant is incarcerated in the Pavilion by the insurgents, the same as his father. He is in the salon now, where the family reside. But he always comes down to the kitchen when he sees Georges arrive. He will be here shortly. We take *déjeuner* together. He is not proud. He is companionable. Ah, I hear his footsteps now.'

Emma and everyone in the kitchen turned to the door which led into the other parts of the house. The door opened and a young man stood in the entrance.

It was Armand. Emma saw Armand before her, yet she could scarcely believe her eyes. Armand was here, in the Pavilion. Part of her search was over. She had found him, at last.

A wave of intense happiness swept over Emma. She could believe her senses now. This was truly Armand walking towards her.

This is not chance. This is not coincidence, Emma told herself. This meeting with Armand seemed to her the culmination of, the fulfilment of her searches in Paris. As she had progressed through the city, she had believed strongly that she would be successful in her efforts. She had not doubted that she would reach Armand, in time. The duke, also, she had been determined to locate. She felt her faith in her quest had been rewarded. Kindly, fate had led her to some solution of her plans. It is more than I deserve, she thought. But Armand is with me now.

Armand was equally surprised to see

Emma. He crossed to her side.

'Emma, my dear, how are you? Is it you, truly you? I thought never to see you again! I thought you, too, had been abducted by the revolutionaries when they took away the Duval family. But you escaped! You are here! Against all the adverse chance in life, we have met up again. Heaven has been with us, indeed, to bring us together again at last! But what is your purpose here at the Pavilion?'

Swiftly Emma told Armand of her mission to see the duke. Then she added, 'I was going to go to the barracks at Boissy-Nord after I had met your father,' Emma assured him. 'How are you Armand? Madame Noelle tells me you are also a prisoner here.'

'Are you two acquainted?' cried Noelle. She faced them with astonishment. Then both Emma and Armand turned their smiling faces to her and assured her that they were friends.

Armand now led Emma down the long corridor towards the front area of the house. They both stopped and faced each other. Armand took Emma into his arms and kissed her with a sweet closeness, a tender and deeply felt emotion.

Emma responded to him. She put her arms around him, to draw him to her. And so they stood, it seemed for a long time, in the enclosure of each other's arms.

Armand took Emma into the salon of the Pavilion. That this had once been an area of beauty and cultured living was obvious, but all its tasteful features had been obliterated or defaced. Everything of value had been removed. There was only a sofa in the middle of the room and a low table before it. What the insurgents could not take away, they had shattered. Curtains had been torn down, mirrors and ornaments smashed, the carpets soiled. A bookcase, cabinet and writing desk had been broken up.

It was the same through the rest of the house. Slogans had been daubed upon the walls extolling the concepts of Liberty and Fraternity. But there was little of either exhibited in the home of the Duke of Rémy and his son.

Emma and Armand returned to the salon and sat together on the settee.

'When I left you at the Château Duval, I returned to Paris as arranged,' Armand began. 'But before I reported to my barracks in Boissy-Nord, I decided to visit my father here at the Pavilion. I found the house in the hands of the revolutionaries and my father a prisoner under close guard. I was at once also taken prisoner and joined my father as a victim and hostage of the so-called Ninth Paris Commune. They are notorious for their violence and unforgiving spirit. My father and I tasted these characteristics at first hand.'

'Did you oppose them?' cried Emma. 'Could you not have defeated them somehow and escaped?'

Armand looked at Emma with amazement.

'But, of course we opposed them! My father and I put up a strong fight! Father is an expert swordsman and he drew his rapier. I was not armed but I used my fists. Alas, it was to no avail. We were outnumbered from the start. They held us off with staves and would not wound or bruise us in any way.

'They are clever. They plan to present us to the people at our trial without blemish. They will take us to be executed in the same way. This will emphasize the fairness of their behaviour. This will make our trial more legal, and the sentence more deserved and more binding.'

Emma sat still, pondering what Armand had told her. She said at last, 'At my home in England, Armand, you were an idealist. I remember how you told us of the plight of the common people of France and how you wished for their lot to be improved. Are you still an idealist, Armand? Do you still hold this view?'

'I am an idealist still,' answered Armand. 'And events have not changed my ideas. I wish for the conditions of the people of France to be changed for the better. But by legal means. By administration, by generosity of spirit. Not by violence and excesses of cruelty and evil.'

'Are these the beliefs and ideas of the Golden Clasp?' Emma asked Armand seriously.

'They are indeed. And these precepts are held by many citizens throughout France. My father and I uphold these convictions. We are proud to be members of this progressive movement.'

It was at this moment that there was a knock at the door of the salon and Noelle entered with a tray on which were two cups of coffee and two slices of freshly cut sultana bread.

At once Emma remembered the croissants in her basket. She chided herself that she had not remembered these before. She opened her basket and drew out the parcel. She kept two croissants for Armand and herself. The rest she gave to Noelle for those in the kitchen, with her compliments.

Emma and Armand now enjoyed this impromptu picnic. The coffee, made from husks and berries, was passable. The currant bread was fresh and the croissants were light.

Emma found that the food gave her new strength. Armand also seemed refreshed. They sat together in companionable silence at the end of their meal. They sat close together. They had no need of words, for their separation and the events which followed had, in a strange way, deepened their relationship with each other. They felt a closer affinity; they felt bound by an emotion that did not need words, that could not be easily expressed.

Finally, Armand said, 'You mentioned earlier that you have with you a letter for my father. Could you hand it to me, please?'

'But no, Armand!' cried Emma. 'I must

deliver this package only to its official recipient, the duke. Please do not be offended. No slur is intended. But I accepted and set myself this mission which I wish to conclude in its entirety. I must hand this letter to the duke, or the whole of my journey and efforts will have been in vain.'

'You are a strange person, Emma!' cried Armand. 'You are stubborn, or determined — I do not know which! But I respect your decision. I was wrong to suggest otherwise. We must both reach the duke, my father. We must go together. There is no other way! It is too risky to wait here for his return.'

'But how can you leave this house?' Emma asked Armand. 'You know it is heavily guarded. Even if by chance we reached the streets and set out to walk to St Ignatius cemetery, you would be recognized. Your face and figure are well known. You could be taken prisoner again. And myself also. I could not bear for this letter to fall into the hands of the insurgents,' cried Emma. 'It would mean the death penalty for us all, without doubt. Also, this communication is important. It is a letter from one king to another,'

Emma resumed. 'It must be delivered, Armand. And intact. I must take it to the duke without hindrance. I feel my honour and my life depend upon this.'

Armand now took Emma in his arms and kissed her.

'I respect your wishes,' he said, 'and your dedication, but how can we escape from this place? How can you safely deliver your letter as you wish?'

For reply, Emma rose to her feet and gathered up the tray which Noelle had brought into the salon.

'Excuse me, please,' she said. 'I must return this tray to the kitchen. I must not trespass on Madame Noelle's kindness again.'

Armand watched her go and saw that Emma had stiffened her shoulders. Her whole mien had changed from the tender informality of their nearness to something quite different. He thought her spine had stiffened, also. Her tread as she crossed the room was purposeful and without fear. He could not see the gleam in her eyes and the straight set of her lips. She smiled as she carried the tray down the long corridor which led to the rear quarters of the house.

She entered the kitchen and saw that they were all seated around the table, enjoying their meal of croissants and fruited bread.

She approached the table and greeted everyone there courteously. Then she stood before them and outlined her plan.

8

Emma sat beside Georges on the driver's seat of the bread van. Before them the horse, Pegasus, trundled his way across Paris through streets, by parks, through the motley crowds of pedestrians.

It was cold perched high beside Georges. Emma was glad she wore her big cloak. She wrapped it around her and drew the hood down to protect her face from the biting wind.

Many people raised their hands to Georges as they went along. But Georges replied with a shake of his head and a gesture with his whip. It was plain that there was almost a famine in Paris now. Food was clearly in short supply for all.

The van was an enclosed vehicle of stout wood and with strong doors. Inside, Georges carried his supplies of bread and cakes which he ferried to his customers. He had some supplies now which he was anxious not to part with. And beside the baskets of bread and cakes, Armand lay, safely covered with clean hessian sacks. He was quite comfortable. He could both breathe and see. He kept quiet as he had been instructed by Georges. He hoped fervently and with all his heart that their coming venture would succeed.

They had had a narrow escape when they had been smuggling Armand into the back of the cart. Georges had backed his vehicle towards the door of the Pavilion's kitchen. Pegasus had been obliging and had shunted the van almost to the door. Armand had entered swiftly and both Emma and Georges had covered him with the sacks.

They had just finished and Georges was manoeuvring the cart out of the courtyard when two guards arrived. These two men had been instructed to take the place of the one guardsman who had been found drunk on duty. They eyed the cart with interest and both stopped.

But Noelle did her part. 'Gentlemen!' she called. 'Guards! I have just made a vegetable stew. Will you step inside my kitchen please and partake of this meal with Emile and myself?'

It was evident that this was an invitation too good to be missed. The two guards entered the kitchen and Georges continued to drive his van out of the courtyard and into the streets beyond.

Georges now began to talk to Emma seriously. By his tone of voice Emma knew that this was a matter of concern to him.

'Our King, Louis, and his wife, Marie Antoinette, are both now prisoners in the palace of Versailles. Oh, there was talk before that they had withdrawn from political life. Perhaps this is true, I do not know. But now they are prisoners, indeed. They are watched day and night by guards and their political masters. The insurgents have gained control. Everything is a political issue, now. Yet, in spite of everything, in spite of the watchfulness of the guards and the vigilance of the spies from the General Assembly, the king and his family managed to escape. Somehow, they procured a carriage, and the king and queen and their family left Versailles and headed away from their home and the capital city. What was their planned destination, I do not know. They carried forged papers. They were travelling incognito. Who they were hoping to meet and where they were to take refuge, I do not know. The whole thing is a mystery. Yet it had terrible consequences.

'After driving for seven hours, the carriage was stopped at a crossing. The royal family were recognized by an ordinary citizen of France — a postmaster at St Meneshould and former dragoon guard of the Condé Regiment. He gave the alarm and the carriage was halted by a mob. The postmaster sent for the National Guard. The soldiers searched the conveyance and took away the forged papers and the letters of alibi.

'And so, the royal family were turned back. They had driven without halting and were well away from the oppression of the communards and the deceit of the National Assembly. Yet they did not reach their destination. They did not fulfil what they had intended to do. Instead, they were escorted back to Paris by soldiers of the National Guard. They were driven through Paris at a slow rate so that the citizens of the capital could see the king and his family return in ignominy and shame. The citizens of Paris expressed their disapproval and indeed condemnation of the actions of the king and queen. They were returned to Versailles, where they are lodged in their own apartments to this day.'

Georges paused now and sank into deep thought. The day was now rapidly declining; it was almost dark. A splatter of rain blew over the bread cart and over the two people high on the driver's seat. Emma was glad again of her cloak and she rubbed her hands against the cold.

Suddenly Georges resumed. 'I am a working man, of course, but it grieves me to think of the king of France being treated in this way. The citizens of France have always honoured their king and queen. It is our tradition. Our conviction. Our way of life. It seems wrong to me that our present king and his consort should be humiliated and disgraced.'

Pegasus seemed to be getting tired, and Emma thought longingly of home. She pictured the Bell House where there was warmth and shelter, with few questions asked.

There was no revolution in England, she thought, no vexed questions of political supremacy. People pursued their ordinary work and family life. Children were taught. Bread was baked in homely kitchens. Sermons were preached on Sunday. Trade went on in a steady way. There was no persecution, no fugitives, no persons accused, sentenced and never seen again.

But Georges was speaking once more. 'This revolution will not last for ever. Eventually peace will be restored to France and legitimate trade begin again. I own my own business. If you are still in France and have not returned to England, I could offer you a position in my bakery business. You have nice hands, nimble fingers. I shall require a young lady to place the crystallized fruits on top of the cakes, mould the almond paste and shape the angelica into leaves. You could also serve in the pâtisserie, meet the citizens of France. Be a little lady with your own domain. But perhaps you will have other ideas,' Georges continued. 'Perhaps you will soon be thinking of a husband and becoming a married lady. I must say, you have a certain charm,' Georges told Emma. 'Though you cut a strange figure to French eyes, with your auburn hair hanging down your back and tendrils round your face! But your grey eyes are round and clear and your figure slim and upright. No doubt some young man will soon present himself and wish to give you his name.'

Emma thought over what Georges had said and decided that she had been paid a compliment.

'Thank you for your comments, Georges,' she said. 'I will bear them all in mind for the future.'

'We are nearly there now,' Georges said. 'The chapel of St Ignatius is nearby. I hope this mission will succeed.'

He paused again. 'In this revolution, many people take sides. Some take more than one side. Some are confused. Some withdraw with horror from the rebellion and its consequences. I take no political sides at the present time. My allegiance now is to the family of the Duke of Rémy and his concerns. My grandfather supplied bread and confectionery to the duke's family, and my father also. I hope to continue this tradition in better times.'

Emma knew that Georges was telling her that he was committed to the success of their coming enterprise. That he would do all he could to help Emma and Armand reach Armand's father, the duke.

With kindly impulse Emma placed her hand over Georges's hand as he held the reins. They pledged themselves together to succeed.

At the gates of St Ignatius' cemetery there was a lodge — a sturdy cabin of wood and glass. Georges halted the cart and they observed the occupants of the lodge. There were three or four communards in there drinking wine, singing and carousing. They had some female company. These women also drank freely and were singing with the men. They waved in a derisive way towards the cart.

Georges and Pegasus stood waiting. For Georges knew that they must have permission to enter the grounds of the cemetery. There was some haggling, but it was finally given.

'Let the bread cart go in! He has no bread inside, that is for sure!'

'No doubt he is taking a short cut through the cemetery to gain the main road to Chantilly. Go on, driver. We cannot mess about searching you in this cold and windy weather. Straight ahead, my man. And good luck to you and your female in the heavy cloak.'

Pegasus moved forward through the avenue of cypresses and heavy trees. The outline of the chapel now stood before them at the end of the drive. A light burned just outside the vestibule and in the rays of this lamp they could see a guard awaiting their arrival.

Emma saw at once that he was a young man, scarcely older than herself. He stood very erect and aware in his uniform of tight trousers, tricolour cap and blue patterned kerchief.

Georges halted the cart and looked down at him. 'Surely I know you, young sir,' he cried. 'Your face is familiar to me. May I ask your name?'

'Pierre Lachasse,' the young guard replied. 'And may I ask your business in this vicinity?'

Georges ignored the question. 'Does your grandmother live near Fontainebleau? I have a revered customer at my bakery with that name and who bears a resemblance to yourself.'

'That is so,' said Pierre. 'But in spite of this acquaintance, I must know your business here.'

Georges got down from his high perch above the bread van. He carried a basket in his hand.

'I have been making a late delivery, and truth to tell I am very tired. My horse is tired, too. We both want nothing more than to reach our home and rest and take something to eat. I shall make no more deliveries today, so I have some edibles surplus to what I require. Would you care to accept this confectionery with my compliments? You would be doing me a favour, for I do not like to see my fresh wares become stale.'

Emma watched Georges lift the cloth from the top of the basket, and inside she saw loaves, a cake, biscuits and a fruit tart.

The young guard, Pierre, stared at this munificence with amazement.

'Why, thank you, sir. How can I repay you? What can I do? You have taken my breath away, sir. I never expected anything like this.'

'Your companions at the lodge will be pleased to share this repast with you. They have wine, I noted, but no food. This addition will make their occasion complete. Why not take this basket to them, Pierre, and share your good fortune with your comrades?'

'I would like to do this, sir, but my orders are to remain here. I must guard this chapel with my life and allow no one to enter or to leave.'

'I will keep watch for you, Pierre,' Georges assured the young man. 'No one disreputable will either enter or leave these premises while I am here. Be off with you! Go along, before I change my mind! It gives me pleasure to reward the grandson of one of my valued friends.'

Both Emma and Georges watched Pierre scuttle off into the darkness. They heard his rapid footsteps along the path and then there was silence.

Georges at once helped Emma down from the driving seat and opened the rear door of the bread van. They both helped Armand to climb out of the conveyance. He was stiff from lying in a cramped space for so long, but soon loosened his limbs and stood upright before them.

Georges also took another basket from the back of the van.

'Those croissants which you gave to us all in the kitchen back at the Pavilion, Miss Emma, were not, if I may say so, of top quality. They were leathery like bread-crusts and without savour. A croissant should be light as a feather, with a buttery taste melting in the mouth. The crumbs should be golden and drift on the air like swansdown. This is a perfection difficult to attain. I have therefore taken the liberty, miss, of placing in your basket some of my own croissants. I trust you will see the difference and enjoy every particle of this gift which is given with my compliments.'

Both Emma and Armand now thanked Georges, not only for his gift of pastry, but for his invaluable assistance to them since they had left the Pavilion.

Georges waved such thanks away. He watched Emma and Armand enter the vestibule of the chapel. He saw the door close behind them and he sighed deeply. He then mounted again to his seat behind the patient and stalwart Pegasus. But neither he nor Pegasus moved away.

Georges continued to keep watch outside the chapel as he had promised the young guard, Pierre.

The wind blew around them and the darkness enveloped them. But Georges sat still, keeping guard, fulfilling his promise to a young man who relied upon his word.

9

Emma and Armand passed from the vestibule of the chapel and entered the main body of the edifice. Emma noticed that the chapel was not large but it was well appointed. It was furnished with rows of dark-wood pews and small stained glass windows. A lamp burned upon the altar giving a dim but steady light. Candles burned also, which warmed the air in the stone walls of this ancient place. The chapel was heavy with the smell of flowers.

Just inside the door Armand and Emma met a young man. The three of them halted and looked at one another. They saw that their new acquaintance was tall and slim with fair hair cropped closely to his head. He wore a long habit of dark cloth and a band of rope around his waist. There were sandals on his feet and a silver cross on a chain around his neck. He spoke to them politely.

'I am Brother Jaime, the sacristan of this chapel. May I ask your business at this late hour in this chapel reserved for those who mourn?' Swiftly Armand identified himself and Emma.

'Your father is keeping an all-night vigil,' replied Brother Jaime. 'He honours his friend and I honour the duke for his compassion and devotion. If you need me, please call my name,' Brother Jaime told them. They watched him retire and knew he was giving them privacy for their meeting with the duke.

Emma saw in the half-light of the chapel, the figure of a man in a central pew. He sat with his head forward in an attitude of contemplation. He did not move. His stillness was complete. Emma knew that before her was her quarry, the man she had sought so fervently, the journey's end of her long and eventful search. She began to move down the aisle towards him.

As she walked forward in this hushed place, a strange emotion swept over Emma. She could not describe it, even to herself. She was filled with a sense of excitement, but more of amazement. She had deeply and intensely believed she would attain her end. And it had truly worked out that way.

It seemed months, even years, since she

had started her quest. She remembered taking those first steps away from the Château Duval, walking along the highway towards Aix-de-Rhône. She recalled seeing Babette and meeting the inn-keeper, and from there being invited to travel to Paris with Maître Barre and Philippe.

She saw before her the strained face of Philippe as he had battled with his malaise; she smelled the oil-of-lavender; she saw the horse chestnut trees in the garden of Chestnut Lodge.

And then the walk next day, through a ruined and shattered city, to the bistro in Rue Poland owned by Sigi Lasard. And then the dreadful meeting with Vincent Giraud, which had so alarmed and distressed her.

She put from her the memory of his touch, his breath, his proximity to the letter she was carrying. She recalled her opposition to him, her conviction that he was not going to defeat her. She heard her footsteps as she ran down the alley towards the square which offered her comparative safety.

It had been a sweet interlude in the square, with water to drink and wash in. And a visit from a cat with doves flying overhead. Then she had moved forward to the Pavilion.

And there she had met Armand. Against all odds, against seemingly high stakes, she had been reunited with the person she cared for, at last. The sweet and tender moments of their encounter flowed over her and for a moment she smiled and her eyes shone.

Then had come the journey with Georges across Paris, with Armand hiding in the back of the bread van. And so to their arrival here.

All this flashed through Emma's mind, mere fragments of recollection. She did not slow her steps until she reached the pew in which the duke was seated. She slipped into the pew beside him and lightly laid her hand upon his arm.

The Duke of Rémy turned towards Emma a face upon which was surprise, amazement even. Emma saw the strong lines of his face, the clarity of his eyes, the broad brow beneath dark hair which waved freely about his head, as Armand's did. Indeed, Emma thought, so Armand will look when he is in his middle years. Determined, self-contained, and yet compassionate and calm.

When the duke saw Armand, he cried out with delight and Emma moved aside so that the two men could embrace.

Swiftly Armand told his father of their escape from the Pavilion and their journey here. And then Armand indicated that Emma should speak.

Emma began, then, to tell the duke of the events which took place before she began her journey. She recounted how Carlo Berlioz, the Italian envoy from the King of Italy, had been entrusted with a letter from the King of Italy to the King of France. She told of how Carlo had been apprehended by the French Government and had had to flee in danger of his life. He had entrusted the letter to Yvette, but she had been unable to undertake the task of delivery due to her seriously sprained ankle. And how she, Emma, had been pressed into service in her place.

The duke listened gravely to her recital. 'And so you, a young girl, travelled to Paris and across the city, alone, and without protection of any kind?'

'It was nothing!' cried Emma. And the duke took one of her hands in his and raised it to his lips.

'And may I take delivery of this letter?' asked the duke.

Emma turned away from the two men so that she could untie the laces on the bodice of her dress in privacy. She drew out the letter and handed it to the duke.

'It is warm!' said the duke with a smile.

'It has been kept safe, sir, I assure you of that.'

The duke opened the parchment envelope and drew out the contents. He spread the pages before him. In the half-light from the altar and the flickering candles, the writing could be plainly seen.

He studied the document without comment. Then he said: 'This letter is, as you have stated, a letter from the King of Italy to the King of France. It is a personal letter, certified to be in the King of Italy's own handwriting. It bears his crest and his initials stamped upon the red wax of the seal. This letter invites the King of France, King Louis, to leave his own country and find asylum and safety in Italy. Look, there is even a map drawn of the route the king should take to leave Paris and proceed to the Italian border. There, this letter states, Italian guards will be waiting for King Louis and his family with conveyances to take them to Rome. They will at all times be under the protection of the Italian guards. No harm will befall them. Their time of trial will be, at the present time, over.

'The King of Italy further states that the revolution in France has alarmed the whole of Europe. Other uprisings are feared. The heads of state in Europe are anxious that some semblance of peace and order must be restored. Also, the departure of King Louis must be seen as a solution to much of the unrest in France at the present time. Much of the dissatisfaction in the country is focused upon the king. If the king were to vanish for a time, the focus of national resentment would be removed. When a more settled atmosphere prevails, then would be the time to discuss King Louis' return. But until then, the King of Italy invites His Majesty King Louis XVI to be his guest at the Royal Palace in Rome.

'All considerations of comfort and convenience will be supplied to the King of France and his family. Italy will be generous in a good cause. The King of Italy presents his compliments to his Majesty, King Louis, and awaits his reply.

The guards are stationed already at the border. The King of Italy urges the King of France to proceed without delay.'

The duke paused and raised his face from his scrutiny of the letter. His voice expressed his urgency and his conviction of the correctness of the course suggested.

He said, 'This letter and invitation also come at a vital time. Perhaps you will have heard, Emma, of the abortive attempt the French royal family recently made to escape? The plan was ill-conceived and badly executed. It seemed to have no rhyme or reason. But this plan you have brought me is more detailed and more exact. It also has the support of the Italian Government with assured asylum at the end of the journey. This document must be delivered to King Louis at once. Without delay. I must gain his approval and put in motion the steps of this arrangement. The king must agree! He must accept! This is the best solution all round! Best for the royal family. And best for the country of France itself!'

The duke's eyes shone. It was clear he was now fully committed to this way forward for the king he served. But Armand sounded a note of caution.

'But nothing can be done now, Father. It is almost midnight. And we are prisoners here. Brother Jaime has just told me that the guards have returned and the chapel is closely patrolled. They intend to take you prisoner tomorrow. And more than that, they are not going to return you to the Pavilion but you will be taken to La Folliatte prison and incarcerated there, until your trial.'

'You are also in danger, Armand,' the duke reminded his son. 'You are an escaped prisoner. They will show little mercy to you when they enter this place tomorrow.'

A shudder of horror passed through Emma as she heard these words. She had heard on her journey through Paris the name of this notorious prison mentioned with hushed breath. There was no return from this place, which was famous for cruelty and its inhumane customs. Emma's heart sank low as she contemplated this fate for the duke, and the man she cared for, Armand.

'We must escape, of course,' said Armand calmly. 'But how?'

'We must escape somehow,' agreed the duke. 'I must go to the Palace of Versailles tomorrow morning. I must accept no delay. My whole life seems to hang upon the letter and its outcome.'

At this moment Brother Jaime appeared, and invited them to proceed to his vestry where he had, he said, just brewed an infusion of herbal tea.

Emma carried her basket also and once in the rather cell-like domain of the sacristan, she raised the lid of the wicker container and they all saw what was inside.

Not only had Georges packed the croissants, as promised, but he had supplied also some patties, biscuits and small cakes.

Brother Jaime had not seen such a feast for a long time and soon the four of them were drinking the welcome hot brew of tea, and enjoying Georges's thoughtfully provided largesse.

Armand had been deep in thought and he now spoke.

'The communard guards at Versailles will be extra vigilant following the king's previous attempt to escape. If the royal family could be persuaded to quit the palace one by one in disguise, that might prove the basis of the plan. The Golden

Clasp will assist with this, Father! There are many wealthy members. They will provide unmarked carriages, clothing, wigs, cloaks — disguises of all kinds! It is only a matter of alerting the members. The Golden Clasp is committed to a peaceful way forward for France. The members will welcome an enterprise of this kind.'

It was now that the duke decided that he must risk taking Brother Jaime into his confidence. He had seen enough of the sacristan to feel he could be trusted. Brother Jaime listened carefully, but could not commit himself.

'I am in an enclosed order,' he said. 'I cannot take part in secular matters. But I will help you if possible.'

It was now that Emma was overcome with sleepiness and a sense of fatigue so intense, she felt she was about to slide off the hard stool she was sitting on and fall to the ground.

'Let us return to the chapel,' the duke said. 'We shall see matters with more clarity in the morning. Let us keep our vigil for Rollo, the three of us. He deserves and would appreciate our devotions for him.'

Back in the chapel it was warmer; the

candles gave out a welcome glow. The duke returned to his pew and bent again in an attitude of consecration.

Emma and Armand took up their places in the pew behind Armand's father. They sat close together in a kind of comfortable proximity. Emma eased off her shoes, for her feet were sore from the walking, and her ankles and calves ached.

Armand placed his arm around her and drew her closer still. And as Emma relaxed against the man she cared for, a sense of peace, ease and happiness filled her. She felt safe and comforted, supported and understood. She experienced a sense of inevitability that they were together, and so drifted off into a peaceful sleep.

Emma woke in the night. She did not know what time it was. Light was beginning to filter through the panes of the stained glass windows. But the candles had burnt out. Only cold wax remained.

Emma saw that Armand had slipped to one side and was lying in an awkward position. Gently she eased her friend upright and supported him with her shoulder. She laid his head against hers and felt the warmth of his breath mingle with her own.

This must be love, she thought, true love; when one wakes in the night and does not think of oneself, but only of the other. When one holds the other in a close embrace, supporting and protecting him, watching over him and tracing the features of his face with sleepy eyes. This must truly be love that endures, that one can rely on, that lasts for ever, she told herself.

Is this love mine? Can I support it? Am I worthy of it? Is Armand's love equal to mine? Equally intense and committed? Emma knew that there would be troubles and trials tomorrow. They were in danger. They must escape. There was much to be done. But she felt she could face anything with Armand at her side. His presence would not only give her courage but would reinforce her devotion and her love.

★　★　★

Brother Jaime awoke them early the next morning. It was scarcely dawn.

He had brewed tea again and they made a hasty toilet and ate the remainder of the croissants for an impromptu breakfast.

Brother Jaime now spoke to them. 'I have considered this matter seriously. I have offered prayers concerning my actions and I am prompted to help you. This chapel was built in the Middle Ages. You can see this from its architecture and the stone walls. It was an age of religious persecution when many atrocities were committed and escapes made. There is a tunnel from the rear of this chapel to the cloisters outside. It has not been used for years but, during the night, I opened it up and inspected it. I found it to be in workable order and fit to be used. I will show you and conduct you to the outside door. This also I have inspected and oiled and made ready for use. This door will open and allow you access to the outside world.'

'Brother Jaime, are you considering what you are doing?' asked the duke. 'When the communard guards enter this chapel to take myself and Armand prisoner, they will find we have gone, and you will be to blame. Their wrath will be vented upon you. You can expect heavy penalties. Your life may be forfeit. Have you thought of this? To aid our escape in this way is a serious step.'

Brother Jaime smiled an angelic smile; his eyes shone, his whole aspect seemed to beam at them.

'Not so, sir. My watch of duty is over in a few minutes and I shall return to the monastery at St Cloud. A relief sacristan will take my place. The guards will not harm a brother who knows nothing of any prisoners, of any escape; who is in ignorance about the events of the night, of any plans put forward, of any unusual activities taking place in this sanctified edifice.

'In any event,' added Brother Jaime, 'the guards are now prostrate with drink from their carousal last night and will not be able to function clearly for some time.'

★　★　★

The tunnel opened off the rear premises of the chapel. It was, indeed, historic and had clearly not been used for many years. Cobwebs clung to the walls; a kind of grey dust hung in the air. There were dead rats upon the floor and other small creatures which had somehow entered this place and had expired there.

Loose stones rattled as they walked; there were pits and cracks in the flooring. Armand put out his arm to help Emma.

She grasped his hand thankfully. She did not wish to fall and be a trouble in this confined space.

But though she welcomed Armand's help, she told herself that she must be self-sufficient. She must stand on her own two feet, whatever happened. She was no helpless female to be cosseted and carried. Perhaps in France there were such females; but in England, Emma told herself, young women were of sterner stuff. She steadied her nerves and walked steadily along the tunnel.

Brother Jaime had gone before them to show the way. They now halted before a large metal door. Emma could see that this had been oiled and cleaned. Brother Jaime took a key and placed it in the lock. The door of the tunnel swung open to reveal the world outside.

Although it was barely dawn and the light was dim, the three of them had to shade their eyes from what appeared to be a sudden glare. They had become accustomed to the gloom of the chapel, and the half-light of the sacristan's cell.

But now, when they stepped outside the confines of the chapel, they found themselves in a small cloister which was heavily wooded and planted with thick shrubs and funereal evergreens.

But beyond the cloister they saw a surprising sight.

There was a long row of carriages draped with black crêpe and hung about with symbols of mourning. The black horses were decked with plumes; their drivers in black livery.

This cortège stood immobile, waiting the word to proceed and leave the cemetery. Brother Jaime spoke with some urgency now. 'This procession is part of the funeral rites of a notability. A man well known in Paris society. He was a member of the National Assembly, but somehow he transgressed the moral code and died in disgrace. His widow decreed that his burial should be as private as possible. The service was held in the chapel yesterday. Perhaps you smelled the flowers, though these were later taken away. The interment has taken place almost in darkness. At dawn, before the light of day.'

Brother Jaime paused, and then indicated a carriage drawn up close to the front of the cloister.

'The other carriages contain mourners but this one is vacant. The family members were overcome and have already returned to Paris. Therefore, please enter this carriage quickly and take your place as mourners of this fallen notability. Sit well back. Do not speak. Hang your heads. Appear overcome with grief. Swiftly now, Miss Emma first, and then you, the duke. And Cadet Armand last of all.'

Rapidly they thanked Brother Jaime, then did as they were instructed. They all attempted to assume the attitude of mourners. Already the front carriages were moving forward. They were just in time to enter the vacant carriage and make their escape.

As this carriage passed through the lodge gates, Emma saw inside the lodge the figures of revolutionary guards still asleep. Empty wine bottles stood beside them.

Then they had reached the open road — the main road which led into Paris. The horses quickened their pace a little as they progressed towards the city centre.

Pedestrians bowed their heads as they passed; the black gauze drapes floated in the breeze. Emma closed her eyes. She felt the danger was over, yet she wondered. Some instinct told her that their safety was a respite only. There were other hazards to face them, ahead.

★ ★ ★

Once well clear of the suburbs, the duke moved in his seat and spoke to the driver. 'Please do not proceed to Paris, but take myself and my companions to the Palace of Versailles.'

The driver half turned towards him. 'I will do that, sir, certainly. My name is André le Brun. I fought with you in the war. I was in your regiment, Captain Rémy. I served you then and I will serve you again, sir. I am honoured to have you in my carriage. Trust me, sir. I will take you to Versailles, safely.'

'I remember you, corporal,' replied the duke. 'I am pleased to meet with you again. Drive carefully and get us there in good time.'

It was now that a mood of nostalgia descended upon Emma. She suddenly longed to see her home and her father, again. She longed to be in the Bell House; to feel its welcoming warmth, the smell of good housekeeping, the comfort of family life.

She remembered the garden which she had loved so well; the village, the church, the local citizens. She loved her father dearly and recalled to herself his face. Even Mrs Kent had suddenly a halo of friendliness and acceptability.

But the duke was speaking to her.

'This office of Gentleman Usher to the King is an hereditary position. My father and grandfather held this appointment before me.'

From these words Emma surmised that the duke was deeply concerned about his coming mission with the king.

'I must succeed,' he said. 'Upon my efforts hang the future of the monarchy and, indeed, the future of France itself.'

Armand also began to speak of the coming plan of escape for the royal family.

'I will see Sigi Lasard to alert the city members of the Golden Clasp. He will be able to mobilize them. He has many resources. He will know how to proceed.'

As if he saw the nostalgia reflected upon Emma's face, Armand placed his arm around her and drew her close to himself. She felt again the reassurance and strength she had sensed emanating from him before. It will be all right, she told herself.

The plan will succeed. Surely nothing can go wrong.

And then they had left Paris behind and had reached their destination.

Before her, Emma saw laid in all its glory and magnificence, the royal residence of King Louis XVI of France and his family.

They had reached the Palace of Versailles.

10

Emma had read about the Palace of Versailles in books back home. For her father, the professor, had not only been a lecturer in English literature, but had had a keen interest in architecture. He had communicated this interest to Emma.

Emma knew that the palace had been built by King Louis XVI upon classical lines with European additions. She knew of the vast acreage it covered; of the rooms, corridors, kitchens, studies, libraries, ballrooms and tennis courts. She had seen pictures of the palisades, the columns, the cupolas, the gardens, the architectural decorations. But nothing had prepared her for the glories of this palace as it lay stretched before her.

The sun had come out and the whole area shone with a kind of golden radiance; the vast pile seemed bathed in a jewel-like light.

Corporal le Brun had drawn up the funeral carriage before the main gates, and Emma saw their metal uprights were gilded, and topped with heraldic shields and other artefacts. Even the Duke of Rémy, who must have seen this palace many times, seemed moved by this occasion. He sighed reflectively before the magnificence which housed the man he served, the king.

Valéry of Rémy now got down from the carriage, smoothed his hair and put his tunic to rights. It was clear he was readying himself to enter the palace and seek this vital audience with King Louis.

Emma and Armand also descended from the carriage. They longed to stretch their legs, for there was little room inside the funeral vehicle. They were also anxious to tell the duke they wished him good fortune and hoped that he would complete his mission without mishap. Both Armand and Emma felt deeply involved in this matter which was now in the duke's hands. They had come so far. But now was the time of completion and this was out of their sphere.

But even as this small party of three stood beside the carriage, speaking to one another words of encouragement on both sides, a platoon of revolutionary soldiers marched to stand in front of the palace gates. They came in military formation, but moved swiftly, taking their places in pre-arranged formations.

Emma stared at these communard guards in amazement. They had seemed to arrive so quickly. They had come from the vicinity of one of the lodge-gates, and beyond. Emma surmised that this rapidity of arrival and formation was part of an overall plan.

She saw also that these revolutionary soldiers were now better armed and were apparently well trained. Many had pistols and rapiers. Hunting guns were in evidence as well as truncheon-like clubs, hung with chains.

The aspect of these soldiers was better, also. They still wore the tight trousers and blue regalia of a united Paris. But they wore these uniforms with pride. As if they had already undertaken many successful manoeuvres and had never been defeated, or thwarted in any way.

And now the ranks of these soldiers parted and their leader advanced through their lines. He stood at last confronting the Duke of Rémy and his small group of onlookers.

This man wore the accepted uniform of

the revolution. He stood with his legs wide apart, in a stance of arrogance and self-confidence.

Emma stared aghast at this man. For it was someone she had hoped never to see again . . .

Vincent Giraud stood at the head of his troops, barring the duke's way forward towards the palace. And, indeed, any obvious route of escape for Emma and Armand.

Vincent Giraud addressed them. 'You, sir, the so-called Duke of Rémy and his poxy son, with that ill-mannered new-comer from England! I have something to say to you, and hear me out you will. You, sir, and your son, disobeyed the sentence passed on you by the Ninth Commune of Paris. You were placed under house arrest at your home. How magnanimous we were! We did not incarcerate you in La Folliatte, or any other prison within the confines of our jurisdiction. And how did you repay us? You escaped from your home and also from the Chapel of St Ignatius. You realize, sir, that this is a flouting of the civic laws of Paris? You have both transgressed against the common people. For the common people are the rulers of Paris, now. We pass the edicts; we keep order. People disobey us at their peril.

'Think on it. For generations the common people have suffered under domination of the land-owners, the usurers, the Royal Court, the corrupt and evil police. But no more. Our time has come and our vengeance against you and such as yourself is complete.'

At this moment there was a cry from Corporal André le Brun. He stood up beside the driver's seat of the carriage and shook his fist at Vincent Giraud and his followers.

'Do you know who you're addressing? Do you know the history of this man? This is Captain Rémy who fought in France's wars. He was wounded, but he discounted his injury. He never speaks of it. No one knows except the men who fought beside him in the last war. Mind your tongue, sir. And do not threaten a man who loves France. Who was prepared to give his life for his country. Without his efforts you would not now be playing soldiers and terrorizing not only Paris, but the surrounding country-side.'

The duke now reached up to touch André on the arm and to forbid him to speak further.

'I do not wish for violence, Corporal. Violence will mend nothing here. Leave me to make my decisions for myself.'

But Vincent Giraud was speaking to them again. They saw he held a pistol in his hand.

'I am now the civic ruler of almost half of Paris. I am empowered to do what I have planned to do. I am going to execute you summarily. There will be no trial. No judge and jury, for all civic authority is now vested in myself. Say your prayers, the three of you! But these prayers will be the last words you utter.'

Vincent Giraud now raised his pistol and levelled it at the duke, Emma and Armand.

A shot rang out, disturbing the doves in the forecourt of the palace, shattering the air with its harshness and explosive quality. But no one standing beside the carriage fell. They were not injured. No bullets had brought them down. They stood immobile, gazing at what had happened before them.

For the person who fell to the ground

with a gunshot wound was Vincent Giraud himself.

He fell forwards into the pebbled and uneven path which surrounded the palace. They could see on his back the lacerations which had torn apart his spine and the upper parts of his body.

Blood ran and spurted from this extensive wound. Blood poured from his mouth; a dreadful spasm shook his body. And then he lay still, drowned in his own blood and with the upper part of his torso almost entirely disintegrated.

The corps of revolutionary soldiers behind him stood motionless, awaiting orders from their new leader. And Valéry of Rémy stood quite still and contemplated the corpse of the man before him.

Valéry of Rémy had been a soldier and had served with distinction in France's armies. But he had never seen the body of a fallen soldier with equanimity and without a sense of diminishment of himself. Every fatality to him was a tragedy. Every death a loss to life and the universe. Every life was, to him, a sacred thing.

And so he gazed with intense regret at the body of the man who only moments before had intended to kill him.

'This terrible war,' he said aloud. 'This dreadful civil war which is tearing France and all its citizens to pieces.'

No one heard these words but Armand and Emma. Emma was herself deeply shocked by the death of Vincent Giraud. He had harassed her. He had perplexed her. But she had never wished him dead. 'No, not that,' she said. 'I never wished to see the end of him like this.'

Tears suddenly filled her eyes. Her throat went dry. I will not fall to the ground, she told herself. I will not faint. I will not reveal these reactions and be a burden to other people. But in spite of herself, she began to shudder. And a spasm of trembling shook her from head to foot.

Armand's face had gone ashen white. He put out his arm to steady Emma and drew her close to himself. She rested against him, glad of his strength and the reassuring warmth of his body.

But now there was a further development in this situation. Again the ranks of soldiers parted and their new leader came forward to take his place at the end of the corps.

Emma saw that the new commander was Léonard Boussac, the second-in-command to Vincent Giraud. The man she had first seen at the Château Duval, when the insurgents had sacked the house and had taken the family prisoner.

His large and burly figure wore a better type of uniform than those of his troops. He wore military decorations and badges of rank. And he carried a pistol in his hand.

This weapon was still smoking from being fired. And in that instant Emma knew that this death of Vincent Giraud had been a political assassination. Boussac, the second-in-command, had shot the acknowledged leader in order to take his place. And Boussac now stood over the body of the fallen Giraud, satisfaction showing on his face.

A burning resentment of horror now filled Emma. She remembered how Boussac had carried little Henri. How Henri had cried out, had appealed to her. But Emma had been powerless to help.

She would have started forward, for all other emotions had now left her. But Armand stayed her and she obeyed his firm but tender touch on her arm.

Boussac now gave orders to his troops, and a body of men came forward and prepared to carry away the remains of their one-time leader. It was a concerted effort. It appeared that the troops had been trained to perform this action. The manoeuvre was swift and effective. The body was lifted and covered. Even a kind of shroud had been prepared which was draped over the figure. Boussac and the followers had intended this elimination. It had been planned. It was an execution. And it was now over.

Boussac paid little attention to the duke, Armand and Emma. He did not address them, or molest them in any way.

His glance on them was malevolent. It seemed to say, *I shall attend to you in due course, when I have time. And when your own time has come, also.*

But for now, Boussac was intent upon clearing the square of troops and the signs of sudden death. His voice rang out commands and the revolutionary soldiers obeyed. They marched away carrying their burden and almost instantly disappeared, leaving the area before the palace gates clear. Except for a pool of blood which glistened in the sun, it was as if the life of

Vincent Giraud had never been.

There was an arbour near to this entrance to the palace which was reserved for those visitors who had not quite gained clearance for their admittance to the inner courtyard. Valéry indicated this to Armand and Emma.

'Take Emma into this garden, Armand,' the duke told his son. 'Emma is almost exhausted and deeply affected. I will try to fulfil my purpose in visiting the palace. I must try to see the king personally, to present to him the letter, and discuss with him what can be done to put the suggested arrangement into actuality.

'I shall perhaps not be long,' continued the duke. 'I might have to leave the letter with the king so that he can discuss the matter with Queen Marie Antoinette. I might have to return later when the whole family had agreed. 'Til you see me again, remain in this arbour. I will return to you both as soon as I can.'

Both Emma and Armand wished the duke good fortune and all speed and success. They watched him walk away towards the palace gates with apprehension. Suddenly the mission seemed threatened and in doubt. Before it had

166

seemed straightforward, but now, after the assassination of Giraud, it seemed chancy and of supreme difficulty. Armand tried to reassure Emma.

'He knows the way, Emma,' Armand said. 'My father knows which entrance of the palace to approach and he knows where the king's private apartments are. He is a trusted confidant. He has served the king well. All the royal attendants know him; he is respected by them all. He will be safe, Emma. Do not fret. Let us go into the arbour and wait for him as he suggested. This way.'

And after a word with André, they both walked away from the palace gate and entered the garden which adjoined the area. This was a pleasant place of shrubs and small trees. There was some statuary and a seat beside a lily pond. Armand and Emma sat down together but, in spite of Armand's efforts at conversation to calm her, Emma's doubts about the duke's entrance into the Palace of Versailles remained.

The palace had looked beautiful in the sunshine; it had seemed gilded with gold, a fairytale palace, a place of harmony and every human delight. But Emma knew that this was not so. For on her walk through Paris, she had heard snatches of conversation which had told her otherwise.

There was no harmony in the palace and few delights left for anyone. The communards were in control and, with the breakdown of civil law which had followed their taking power, an equal breakdown in conventional morality had taken place. Wild orgies were held in corridors and the beautiful reception rooms were the scenes of licentious parties. This laxity had deeply offended both the king and the queen.

But Emma tried to put these dark thoughts from her. She began to talk to Armand, trying to lighten the atmosphere between them.

'What will your plans be, Armand, when this civil war is over? Have you thought so far? Please let me know.'

'I must finish my tour of duty with the Corps Royale at Boissy-Nord. I shall also help my father with the administration of our estates. We have farmlands near Marseilles and forests in Provence. When peace is restored these must be administered. Until that time, I shall fight for my beliefs under the auspices of the Golden Clasp.

'And what of yourself, Emma? What are your future plans?'

'I must return to England and help my father with his university work. I have my own studies to finish. But somehow, after being in France and living through this part of the revolution, essays and poetry seem to have lost their charm. Perhaps I shall find more interest as time goes on.'

Armand fell silent and Emma said, 'In your heart, you are afraid for your father in the palace, are you not, Armand?'

'Yes. Everything has changed. He goes into danger. And if he does not return, we shall have no redress. For the communards rule there with an iron hand, even dictating the terms of his daily life to the king. They will have little mercy upon a Gentleman Usher who is known to oppose their regime and their reign of terror and cruelty.'

Emma took Armand's hand. She tried to lighten the situation a little and take Armand's mind off his father's mission.

'It is my birthday next week, Armand. I shall be sixteen!'

'It was my birthday a month ago. I am now eighteen.'

'We are almost middle-aged, Emma. We are like a settled pair of ancient married folk!'

The nearness of our birthdays seems to draw us closer together, Emma thought.

Armand suddenly spoke to her seriously.

'I love you, Emma,' he said.

'And I love you, too, Armand.'

And as she spoke, as she realized the depth of their commitment inherent in these simple words, a new sensation of strength and purpose coursed through her. I can do anything if I have his love, she thought. I can endure and not complain and shape a happy future for us both. I did not realize that love was like this. That it was strengthening and gave direction, reinforcing one with its unusual power.

She turned her face to Armand and he drew her closer. He kissed her with gentle intensity and she responded to his embrace. They sat in total silence now, just holding hands and being close to each other.

Emma guessed that there were more

events to come and she must be ready to face them. She had not long to wait. For after about an hour's time, the Duke of Rémy returned to them in the arbour.

They knew at once he had bad news. He was downcast and in a state of wariness and a mood of haste.

'I managed to get into the palace,' he told them, 'and progressed as far as the entrance to the king's private apartments. But there I was stopped. Not by an insurgent, but by an old and trusted adviser to the king I knew well. He told me that the king had already left Versailles. He had been taken from the palace by the revolutionary guards and secured in a lodgement close to the guillotine. Bertrand, this courtier, begged me not to enter the main rooms of the apartment, for if I did so I would myself be taken prisoner and also taken to this same jail, or La Folliatte, from which there is no return.

'Bertrand took a message for me to Queen Marie Antoinette, suggesting that she, herself, should quit the palace under the auspices of the Golden Clasp. But she sent word back at once that she would not do this. She did not wish to leave the king.

She knows her days are numbered and that she will shortly join her husband at this dreadful annexe to the guillotine. One can only admire her courage and strength. She has been criticized, but now she reveals herself as a woman of dedication and strong purpose.

'After Bertrand had urged me to go, I left the palace as quickly as I could. My only consolation in this abortive mission is that I still have the letter intact. The letter from the King of Italy to the King of France is still safely in the pocket of my tunic. It did not fall into the communards' hands, which would have been a disaster. At least that letter is secure. At least no confidences have been betrayed and the king's own personal condition made worse.'

'So we have failed, Father, is that it?' asked Armand.

'We have not failed, Armand. We have carried out our designated part of the mission as we expected of ourselves and others, and as best we could. Circumstances altered to make the completion of our plan impossible. There is no shame in that. History will judge us. We cannot judge ourselves. At least we three are together and we have not lost our lives.'

And now the duke began to speak earnestly, and with haste. 'We must quit this place at once. Believe me, there is no margin of safety in our presence here. Boussac is certain to return for us. I know his intention. He will deal with us as he dealt with Vincent Giraud. Come, let us go back to the carriage, and rejoin André.'

Emma and Armand now stood and followed the duke from the arbour.

'But where shall we go to?' cried Armand. 'We cannot return home! But we have no other lodging place to hand!'

The duke seemed taken aback by this statement. They stood by the carriage in uncertainty, not knowing where to direct André to drive.

But Emma smiled. I have a home in Paris. I have a base, she told herself. Maîitre Barre offered me his hospitality for as long as I remained in France. She was certain he would receive the small party.

'I know where to go!' she cried. 'And I will direct André there. To Chestnut

Lodge, on the Rue Chantain, in the suburb of Annecy. To the home of Maîitre Barre and Philippe Barre. We will all take refuge there! We shall be safe there with my friends.'

11

The carriage gathered speed and moved swiftly away from the environs of the palace. Emma sat between the two men in the place she had occupied before.

The duke sat with his head bowed. He was clearly disappointed that his mission had not borne fruit. He had not been able to serve the king as he had wished. Matters had moved out of his hands, rendering his efforts abortive.

Armand seemed abstracted, also. He looked out of the carriage window at the passing scene but did not say a word. Emma knew that he was concerned not only about his future when the civil war was over, but about his next movements with the Golden Clasp.

There must be a way forward for him, Armand was certain. But what that was at the moment he did not know.

Emma sat very still. In spite of the inconclusiveness of their intentions, she felt some measure of comfort and peace. Perhaps my time here is drawing to a close, she thought. Perhaps I have now done all I can, and not a great deal more is expected of me. Again she felt an intense desire to see her father and her home in England. She longed suddenly for the peace of the Cambridgeshire countryside, the study where her father worked, the ancient peace of Cambridge and the river nearby.

She was so engrossed in her own thoughts that it was some time before Emma realized that there was something wrong in the carriage. Things were not as they had been before. Something had changed, and something vital, something important to themselves and their journey.

She scrutinized the interior of the carriage, and then her eyes settled upon the figure of André, their driver. But André had changed. Before he had been a tall, thin man, no longer young. But the man now driving this coach was broader, taller and, Emma could see, younger in every way. She touched the duke lightly on the arm to rouse him from his introspection. His eyes also followed Emma's direction towards the substitute coachman.

The coach had now entered the Bois, a

strip of cultivated forest which ran through this area of the city. Tall trees made an avenue of shade. Bushes lined the pathways and evergreens added to the density of the foliage. It was a pleasant area which suggested peaceful walks and gentle pursuits. But it had another reputation, also. This area abounded with footpads, robbers and miscreants of all kinds. And the carriage had penetrated into this wooded glade.

Armand was alerted now, and they were none of them surprised when the carriage stopped.

The coachman turned in his seat and regarded them with a cool smile. Emma saw his eyes glitter and guessed that this was a moment of triumph for him. This was something he had waited for, and relished now it had taken place.

The passengers in the coach were astonished to find they were looking at the face and form of Carlo Berlioz.

Carlo Berlioz!

He had passed out of Emma's mind as soon as she had left the Château Duval. Yvette had said he had returned to Italy. And yet he was here. Now. And he was clearly holding them in ambush.

'I see you are surprised to see me,' the Italian envoy said. 'And you are going to be equally surprised at my purpose.'

'And what is your purpose, sir?' asked the duke. 'I do not take kindly to your intrusion. And what of my corporal? Where is André le Brun? How have you dealt with him?'

'Your corporal is safe. We merely exchanged uniforms. Under duress, unfortunately. As you see, I am now garbed as a funeral attendant, while André le Brun wears my civilian suit. The corporal is unharmed and you will see him again. But that is a minor matter. My purpose here with you is of great importance to us all. Important to Italy,' he said. 'Important to France. And important to myself.'

'Kindly do not bandy words further,' replied the duke. 'State your terms and conditions and let us be on our way.'

'The letter,' Carlo Berlioz said. 'The letter from the King of Italy to the King of France. That is my objective. And that is what I must obtain. This missive is one of the most vital letters ever penned, and it is in your hands. I demand, Valéry of Rémy, its return.'

'Certainly not,' answered the duke. 'No

document of any kind will be handed to you. You have no authority. You have no legal cause. No one here will yield to your terms. Quit this carriage at once and let us be on our way.'

'That letter is my own property,' reiterated Carlo Berlioz. 'It was brought into France from Italy by myself. It was entrusted to me by the Italian Government. You have no rights to it whatsoever and I demand its return.'

'That letter was addressed to myself,' answered the duke. 'It was not your private property. You were only the postal carrier, the go-between. That letter was never your personal possession. And I will never hand it to you under duress.'

'It was truly the king's property,' Armand now spoke. 'He was the designated recipient. My father will keep the letter on behalf of His Majesty, guarding it as proxy to the king.'

'If you will not be reasonable, I shall have to use force,' said Carlo Berlioz. And they saw that he held a rapier in his hand.

He did not speak for a few moments. He let them see the thin and cruel blade, silver sharp, with its devastating point and long-handled thrust.

His smile widened, his pleasure in this moment increased. He pointed now the weapon not towards the duke, or Armand, but towards Emma. The tip of the blade almost touched her breast.

'You did well, Emma,' he said, 'to undertake the commission from Yvette and travel into Paris, across the city, seeking the Duke of Rémy. And against all the odds, all chances, you succeeded in locating your quarry. You fulfilled your mission without discovery or mishap. Where another person more mature, more sophisticated, might have failed, you with your innocence and youth won through. A tribute to England, though it is a land I loathe.'

'I do not wish for your commendation, sir,' replied Emma. 'And I find your final comment offensive.'

'You, with your bizarre appearance, have charmed these two men, did you know?' continued Berlioz. 'One loves you. The other approves you, so much is obvious. But if my demands are not accepted and agreed, no other men will look upon you with favour in the future. For this blade will pierce you, and all your attractions and your life will ebb away.'

'No!' cried Armand. His voice shattered the silence in the carriage. 'No. Do not touch Emma! She must not be harmed. Kill *me* if you must, but not Emma. I shall defend her with my life! You must kill me first before you harm her!'

Armand stood up, and interposed himself between Carlo Berlioz and Emma. The tip of the rapier touched his shoulder, but he did not move.

And then Armand spoke again. His voice rose and he seemed in the grip of some great emotion, some cataclysm of intention. He cried, 'Give Berlioz the letter, Father. Hand it to him. Death or wounding is not worth defiance. If you will not give him the letter, I will take it from you.'

And Armand turned, leaned over his father, and undid the fastening of his tunic. He appeared to abstract the document from the inner pocket of the duke's jacket. But in reality he undid the fastening of the duke's leather belt, and grasped it in his hand. Then, with one wild encircling movement, Armand whirled around. In a fast parabolic arc the leather belt flew out. The metal clasp of the belt shot through the air, gaining momentum, a weapon in its own right. The clasp hit the arm and shoulder of Carlo Berlioz, knocking the rapier out of his hand.

He cried out with surprise and pain as the leather of the belt encircled him. Berlioz himself now lost his balance and fell from the seat of the coach on to the grass verge of the woodland. He lay still, the broken rapier at his side.

Armand at once jumped down from the carriage and inspected the body of Berlioz. 'He is not seriously hurt,' he said. 'Winded and bruised. But nothing more.'

'Leave him to recover in his own time,' the duke advised. And Armand mounted to the high seat of the driver and took up the reins of the startled horses.

'But I do not know the way!' Armand cried. 'Where is this house? Where is this suburb of Annecy? Advise me! Give me directions, please!'

'I know the way,' cried Emma. And without more ado she got out of the carriage, lifted her skirts, and climbed up to the driver's perch to sit beside Armand.

'Straight ahead through the Bois and turn left,' Emma said. For she had correctly surmised that the Bois ran parallel to the course she herself had taken, during her long walk to Armand's home, the Pavilion.

The horses were glad to feel the reins in safe hands again and trotted briskly away.

I am becoming accustomed to this high position in Paris! Emma told herself, as she looked down upon the tree branches and shrubs of the forest as the carriage moved steadily forward. Firstly on a baker's bread cart, and now on a funeral carriage!

She laughed aloud and Armand turned to her with a smile. And so they found the main road and headed towards Annecy, and Chestnut Lodge.

* * *

If, later that afternoon, Maîitre Barre saw Emma arrive at his home as part of a funeral cortége, the reins in the hands of a strange young man, he did not show his surprise. He received Emma cordially, and was gracious and hospitable towards Armand and the Duke of Rémy. As soon as the lawyer knew the circumstances of their arrival, he offered the two men the full use of his home and pledged to assist them in any way that he could.

He took Emma aside. 'I am truly gratified to see you again, Emma. Believe me, I have been deeply concerned for you. I knew your errand was important, though you did not describe it to me. You did not take me into your confidence. But soon I began to realize that your mission was also dangerous. That your commission was taking you into a vortex of events which might prove overwhelming for you. You might not realize the dangers. You might receive greater penalties for which you were not prepared.'

'But I have been safe, Maîitre Barre!' cried Emma. She felt deeply touched by the older man's concern. 'And I am glad to see you again. And Philippe also.'

Philippe embraced Emma, but in an enthusiastic way. She thought he was looking in better health already. There was a glow of colour upon his face. He told her he was pursuing his studies steadily and was already helping his father in the legal chambers.

And now there was a great deal of activity in the household. Rooms and beds were prepared for Armand and his father. Meals were hastily concocted; toilet articles and other amenities were produced and offered to the guests.

Arlette flew about, glad of the unusual activity, and to be serving such honoured guests. She took Emma aside.

Arlette had a small private cubicle at the rear of the kitchen. In this she kept her own personal requisites for her toilet. There was a tin bath, hot water, soap, flannels. She filled the tub with water and withdrew. Emma had not realized how much she had longed for this bath. She stripped off swiftly and stepped into the warm water. She bathed herself and washed her hair. She towelled it dry, so that it hung down her back in a dark, auburn cascade.

Arlette fetched her a change of under-wear and her other dress. And so, refreshed and hungry, Emma entered the dining-room for the early evening meal. This was not a convivial meal, but a pleasant one. A sense of relief of tension filled the air. Wine was offered and the food enjoyed. It seemed that dire events were passed.

Philippe aided his father in his expressions of hospitality. Emma knew that part of Philippe's efforts were to repay his debt of friendship to herself. She greatly appreciated Philippe's thought and attentions. He also clearly liked Armand, and the two young men were soon on easy terms. The duke and Maître Barre talked together. These two older men of experience and authority were able to talk without preliminaries. Emma knew that each accepted the other without question or demur.

At the end of the meal when the dishes had been cleared, the duke began to speak to them all. He came straight to the point of the vital matter which concerned them.

'It had been known for some time, in political and diplomatic circles, that Carlo Berlioz was a double agent, serving both the Italian and French Governments. He had many contacts and informers. When he learned that I had been unable to deliver the letter to King Louis he saw an opportunity to advance his own purpose. He decided to enrich himself, and make his own future independent and secure. He realized that this letter, undelivered, was a prize of inestimable importance. What would not the government of Austria pay to possess this document? Germany? Catherine of Russia? And your own country, Emma, Albio, across the sea?

Or could he threaten the Italian Government itself with general disclosure of the contents of this missive? The Italians might pay dearly to receive back this incriminating document to avoid embarrassment, or condemnation of meddling in another nation's affairs.

'In any way, Berlioz believed he had the means to hold Europe to ransom. He saw monetary gains for himself, as well as a brilliant future. Had he succeeded in his plan, the results would have been disastrous. Nothing less than the disruption of the balance of power in Europe. A total war might have resulted. And the civil war in France spread further afield, enveloping other nations in a dreadful conflict.'

The duke paused and Armand asked, 'What now, father? Now that Berlioz has been defeated and disarmed?'

'This letter must be returned to the King of Italy without delay,' replied the duke. 'It must not be read or discussed. It must be kept strictly private until it is handed over to its originator, Italy's own king.'

'And how will you effect that, sir?' asked Maître Barre.

'This letter is addressed to myself, in the

king's own hand. It is therefore my responsibility to personally return the letter to His Majesty. I will journey into Italy, following the route suggested on the map enclosed within the letter. This route charts the way through France to the Italian border. There, Italian guards are waiting to receive the reply from King Louis. I will then explain the position and journey with the Italian guards to Rome. I shall guard this letter with my life and regard this mission as of great military and political importance.'

'You will need a powerful horse,' said Maître Barre reflectively. 'I have my own stables but my horses are for the personal use of myself and Philippe only. I do have a friend — a member of the Golden Clasp — who has a livery stable and also keeps strongly-bred horses for his own hunting enjoyment. I know he will aid us. I will see him this evening and make arrangements for your departure.'

'Tomorrow,' added the duke.

And Maître Barre said, 'Yes, I will make all arrangements for you to leave tomorrow.'

'How can we help you, Father?' Armand asked.

'I want you to go to Versailles to try to find Corporal André le Brun and make sure he is safe. It grieves me to think of him being mistreated by Carlo Berlioz.'

'And Emma!'

'Yes, sir?' answered Emma.

'I would like to suggest that you now return home to England. I believe your tour of duty here in France is now over. The Duval family are missing and can offer you no further employment. Armand must return to his duties with the Corps Royale at Boissy-Nord, and Maître Barre and Philippe have their own occupations to pursue. I believe your father and thoughts of home now occupy your mind. I suggest you leave France shortly and make your way back to England. Do you agree?'

Emma nodded her head. She was speechless. She had longed with all her heart to suggest that she should now return home. But she had not wished to appear a coward, unable to face up to further events. She did not wish to appear selfishly wrapped up in her own concerns.

But for the duke (who was clearly now in charge of their future course of action) to give his blessing to her departure, eased her way forward, and her words of acceptance.

'I will go at once to try and find the corporal,' Armand said.

'And I will accompany you,' added Philippe.

'Take the family coach!' cried Maître Barre.

And Armand added, 'I will return the funeral carriage to its rightful owners, also.'

So in all this flurry of future arrangements, Emma said goodnight and went upstairs.

She heard the sounds of horses' hooves and carriage wheels, and then there was silence. She got into bed and was soon fast asleep.

★ ★ ★

During this night, Emma had a dream. Yet it was more than a dream. It was a re-creation of the events which had taken place in the funeral carriage late that afternoon, in the Bois.

She remembered the moment when Carlo Berlioz had turned to face them, when he had revealed his true identity and his purpose. When he had demanded the letter and had drawn his rapier to reinforce his demands.

She remembered how the point of the blade had almost touched her breast. It had brushed Armand's shoulder. But it had been intended for herself.

It had been a stratagem, what had occurred next. Armand's cry to the duke to hand over the letter. The pretence of bending over the duke to take the letter, but in reality to unwind the strong leather belt with the metal clasp.

She saw again the arc of the belt as it flew through the air, uncoiling itself like a snake. And then the cry of pain and outrage as Berlioz was knocked off balance and his rapier broken. He had lain prone on the grass verge, clearly unconscious.

She heard in the stillness of the night Armand's cry that Berlioz should kill himself rather than her. It had not been a gesture for show. No play-action. No ruse or artifice. Before, in the arbour, Armand had expressed his love in words. But in the carriage his words had been reinforced by action. Armand had offered his own life forfeit for hers, from a depth of love she had only glimpsed before but had never thought to experience.

She got out of bed and walked to the window of her room. She looked outside. She did not see the gardens of the Bell House, and the distant village. She saw the inner courtyard and the curving tiles of the Parisian roofs.

The moment of realizing the extent of Armand's caring for her, through his willingness to offer himself for her, was the pinnacle of her experience in France. But more than that, she thought, this vital moment was the climax of her life, so far. What had gone before had led up to this. This was the culmination of her present existence. Beyond that, she could not go.

She thought that perhaps there would be other vital moments in her life: marriage, her family, material or personal success. But none will ever touch this, she told herself. The moment when she realized how deeply Armand loved her would always be supreme.

She got back into bed and was soon asleep. She slept peacefully, already fortified to face the days ahead and the events which were to come.

★ ★ ★

The next morning when she went downstairs, Emma found a newcomer in the hall. It was the Corporal André le Brun. He greeted Emma warmly and seemed in good spirits.

'I was sorry, miss, not to have been able to defend you in the Bois, but that miscreant Italian had knocked me out and had stolen my uniform. He had impersonated me! What an impertinence. But he has disappeared now. I do not know where he is. I have returned with Cadet Armand and have offered my services to his father, the duke. I understand a journey is being arranged when we will ride together as we used to.

'I am a cavalryman, miss, as is the duke. We know and understand horses. I will attend the duke on his mission and will be glad to be in his service again. I am a widower now and have no home responsibilities. So I can be absent from Paris, as required. Believe me, miss, the duke will be safe in my company. We have served in doubtful situations before and have come through victorious. And so we will this time, without doubt.'

And now there was a flurry of preparations and departures. It had been arranged that Armand should escort Emma to Boulogne, to try to catch the packet there. Philippe had volunteered to drive the carriage and so the three friends prepared to depart.

Emma was genuinely sorry to say adieu to Maître Barre and Arlette. Their kindness had been very heart-warming for her. She hoped sincerely to see both of them again.

'I trust I did not embarrass you, bringing members of the Golden Clasp to lodge under your roof, Maître. I know you valued your neutrality. I trust I did not offend.'

'On the contrary, my dear. I left the middle way of life without regret,' answered the lawyer. 'To take a middle course through events leads nowhere. I am committed now to the Golden Clasp and its aims for progress for France through legal and constitutional means.'

Emma and Armand sat in the coach, while Philippe drove the carriage. They spoke little but sat close together. Both knew that events had said all for them. Words were not necessary now to reinforce their caring and commitment to each other.

Armand knew also, in those moments in the Bois when he had opposed Carlo Berlioz and had placed his life in jeopardy, that he had revealed to Emma the deep places of his heart and nature. Both were bound together now in their memories of this.

Emma asked that they should take a round-about way to the seaport. She requested that they should drive firstly to the Golden Pheasant at Aix-de-Rhône, to see Babette and her father, Pierre Marachel.

'Emma! You have returned! And you have a charming fiancé! A cadet in the Corps Royale!' cried Babette. And her father busied himself to bring them coffee and wine, and to attend to the horses.

After this visit, Emma asked to be driven to the Château Duval. A place of pleasant memories, tinged with sadness, as she recalled the catastrophe which had, at the end of her stay, befallen the entire family.

As they approached the château, Emma saw, to her surprise, that some of the farms were being worked and had been put in order. The approach to the château also was orderly; the drive swept, the gardens cared for.

Followed by the two men, Emma went up the stone steps which led to the front entrance. She tried the door, now repaired and repainted. The door opened and she entered the château.

The hall was devoid of furniture, as she had expected. But it was very clean and tidy. They walked along the hallway, and then, as before, Emma heard voices.

She crossed the hall to the door to the kitchen and knocked. She opened the door and went down the steps into the kitchen.

It was as if she had never been away. Hélène was there, and Yvette, and a tall, well-built man who Emma knew to be Léon, Hélène's husband. They stared at the three visitors in amazement, and then cries of welcome rang out, questions, explanations, all the conversation of those who had been parted and who were now reunited.

'You must stay for our meal!' Hélène cried. 'I have just baked bread. There is barley soup with a ham bone and a custard made from eggs and cinnamon!'

'Léon has returned to me, Emma. We were separated before. But now this is our home and we are caring for the château and what has been left of its possessions, together.'

'Emma!' cried Yvette. 'Were you able to fulfil the commission? Did you reach the duke? Did he present the letter to the king?'

Emma now told Yvette what had occurred. She was disappointed, but glad that the threat inherent in the letter was being rendered harmless by the duke.

Emma saw that Yvette's leg was causing her pain. Her face was swollen also, and red. She had clearly recently been crying.

'It is because of Carlo Berlioz!' cried Yvette. 'He deceived me, Emma. All his promises meant nothing. It was a fantasy which I took as the truth. There was no betrothal. No future life in Rome. No marriage. Nothing. He left me without a word, a hope, an explanation. He was a married man, Emma. And he has vanished. I do not know where he is. My cousin in Paris told me the truth. And now he has totally disappeared.'

Swiftly Emma and Armand told Yvette of the events in the Bois. She was further horrified to know of her former lover's treachery. But this did not heal her wounds.

She began to weep again. And then a strange thing happened. Philippe crossed to Yvette's side, and said, 'Mamselle, your distress will pass. We all suffer reverses but, with courage, matters often turn out better than we expect. Look, take my arm. Let us take a stroll in the garden. The fresh air will revive you. You can recount to me your troubles and this will ease the pressure on your mind. This way. I will support you, for I can see your ankle is still weak.'

At once Yvette dried her eyes and smoothed her hair. She rose to her feet, and gracefully took Philippe's arm. They began to walk through the kitchen together, to the rear door which led into the outer grounds.

'And you must tell me about yourself, sir,' Yvette was saying. 'I welcome your acquaintance and hope for your friendship.'

Emma saw her two friends leave the kitchen and make their way along the path she remembered so well: the walk which led to the woodland, and the arbour and gazebo.

'We have had no news of the count and countess,' Hélène was telling Emma. 'Or

Henri. Our lives seem bereft without them. We will keep the château ready for their return.'

Hearing these words, Philippe re-entered the kitchen with Yvette. He repeated the name, '*Henri*?'

'Henri?' he said again. 'And this is the Château Duval?'

'It is indeed,' replied Hélène. 'Have you news of Henri?'

'I have indeed. And how could I have forgotten to tell you? I have become the trustee of an orphanage in Paris,' continued Philippe. 'And while I was there only yesterday, a young boy approached me and identified himself as Henri Duval. He had just been admitted. He said his parents had been captured, taken from their home and driven into Paris by cart. Once there, his parents had urged him to escape. They implored him not to regard themselves, but to jump from the cart and vanish in the streets of Paris. And this, obeying them, he did.

'He lived for a short time with one of the bands of abandoned and marauding children, which are such a problem now in Paris. But then he was taken into the orphanage where he is lodged at the moment. The young boy mentioned you, Emma. I recall this now! And told me of your kindness, and that he longed to see you again.

'Henri impressed me,' continued Philippe. 'And I asked the patronne of the orphanage to grant him extra care and attention. I left the patronne ample funds for this.'

Tears flooded into Emma's eyes as she heard this account of Philippe's meeting with Henri. Dear little Henri was safe!

Philippe had concluded, 'I shall go to see the young boy, Henri, again, when we return to Paris.'

Yvette and Emma decided to take a stroll in the garden while Hélène prepared a meal for everyone.

'What are your plans now, Yvette?' asked Emma.

And Yvette replied, 'I have no plans at all. I have no work. I have no money. I cannot trespass upon the kindness of Hélène and Léon for much longer. But where to go and what do to, I do not know. My ankle troubles me continually and I am overwhelmed with depression. I tell you all this, Emma, not from a sense of self-pity, but in an attempt to face facts and consider the realities of my life.'

'Would you care to come back to England with me, Yvette?' asked Emma. 'You could spend several months with us all at the Bell House and recover your health and sense of direction. You were part of the family before. You know our routine and way of life. You would be welcome, I am sure. Yvette, say you will come! I would love to have your company again.'

'But I have no money!' cried Yvette. 'How can I pay my fare on the boat to England?'

'The Duke of Rémy has provided for me well in this direction,' replied Emma. She had been reluctant to accept the proffered gift from the duke, but he had insisted.

'You have earned this by your services to my family, Emma,' he had told her. 'And Armand wishes you to be provided for as you journey back to England.'

Hélène now called them all to their meal, and with so much solved it seemed in happy fashion, a mood of pleasure and elation gripped the whole company.

It was towards the end of the meal that Léon cried, 'Wine! We must have more wine!' And he rose from the table and made his way across the kitchen towards the trap-door which led to the cellar below.

This trap-door was of stout construction, situated against the far wall. Below was the dungeon-like area which housed the wines, the vegetables and the wood for the household fires.

Léon hoisted the trap-door open and went down the steps into the underground chamber. They heard his footsteps on the stone steps and distantly the chink of bottles as he selected the wine.

It was at this moment that the main door of the kitchen opened and a man entered the room. He was stoutly built with a fresh complexion and bronze-coloured hair. He wore the uniform of the insurgents, with the blue and white insignia of this revolutionary band. He wore also a sword in its scabbard around his waist.

Yet there was something different about the uniform upon this man, a sense of style. The evidence of good material and polished leather gave an impression of good living and ample funds. He stood still and surveyed the scene, and them all.

It was Boussac.

'So, you did not expect to see me again!' he cried. 'Nor I you! We have not met since the occasion at Versailles where Vincent Giraud met his destined end. I remember also the first time I entered this château, when the count and countess were taken prisoner. I liked the place then and at that time decided it should be mine, that I would make it my home.'

'Who are you, sir?' cried Hélène, who had risen to her feet. 'I do not know you. You are an intruder and not welcome here. Begone, sir, without delay.'

'You must be the housekeeper,' said Boussac, advancing into the centre of the room. 'I shall require your services, madam, when I am in residence. And also the services of the young people here, who will be my minions to minister to my needs.'

Armand now confronted Boussac. 'No one here will serve you, sir. We would die rather than become your servitors.'

'Fine words! A show of defiance! But you will all become the prisoners of the revolution and subject to my will. Better than the guillotine, I believe.'

Boussac now removed the belt from his

waist and tossed his sword and scabbard on to a chair near the table. It was a gesture of defiance to them all and a movement which seemed to reinforce his taking of the château as his home.

And now a voice rang out in the suddenly silent kitchen.

'Léonard Boussac,' Philippe said. He had risen to his feet and repeated the name again. 'Léonard Boussac. I would have known you at once. And we meet again after this long time.'

Philippe left his place at the table and faced Boussac. 'You have been in my mind for years, you and your evil deeds. We were students together at the academy and you tormented me, humiliated me, destroyed my confidence and power to function and live. You added fuel to the fire of my illness. I seemed unable to withstand you. But I can withstand you now.'

Philippe began to walk towards Boussac. 'I was afraid of you before but I am not afraid of you now. And I shall never be afraid of you again.'

No one knew exactly what Philippe planned to do, how he was going to revenge himself against Boussac, if that was in his mind. Philippe was not armed, but on his face shone a confidence and certainty that gave him authority.

Léonard Boussac was taken aback by Philippe's appearance, his words and his mien. Instinctively he shrank away, and so he approached backwards, the open trap-door which led to the cellar.

At this moment Léon appeared from the cellar, bearing two bottles of wine. He was startled, seeing the figure of Boussac looming above him. He stumbled and the wine fell, the bottles shattering on the kitchen floor.

Boussac half spun round at this commotion. He was trapped between Léon and Philippe, unable to escape. He tried to regain his balance — lurching this way and that. And then with a wild and desperate cry, he fell backwards into the open maw of the château's cellars. He disappeared with a cry of rage and dismay into the blackness below.

No one had laid a finger on Boussac. His death was an accident many thought he had brought upon himself. But they heard his bulk hit the stone steps, his limbs and head break against the stone walls. They heard his frantic cries die away at last into silence.

Léon acted swiftly. He descended at once into the cellar. They heard his movements below. When he re-appeared in the kitchen his face was ashen grey.

'There has been a fatality,' he said. 'Boussac is dead. We must act swiftly. His followers, his cohorts, will be here shortly. They always follow their leader. We must remove the body and all traces of Boussac's visit. This château must be as if he has never appeared here. The two men, Armand and Philippe, assist me, please, to remove the body from the château. The young ladies, prepare to leave at once.

'Hand me his sword and scabbard, Armand. Hélène and I will bury the body later; the sword with the cape. Boussac's horse will be ridden away and given to a nearby farmer.'

All did their part, urgency lending speed to their actions.

'Hélène will provide food for the journey to the coast. Your horses are rested and watered. I pray you, speed away. I pray God be with you on your journey and that you will travel unmolested.'

'Will you be safe?' cried Emma.

'How can we leave you unprotected and alone?' added Armand.

'We are survivors,' said Léon. 'We can hold our own here. With Boussac gone there is nothing to incriminate us. We shall win through. Now, God speed and bless you all.'

★ ★ ★

The four friends reached Boulogne in good time, after travelling through the night without incident or mishap. Two passages were available on the ferry and until then they explored the town and strolled upon the quay.

'You are still concerned for your father,' commented Emma to Armand.

'He will be safer now the corporal rides with him,' replied Armand. 'But it is his return to Paris that perplexes me greatly. We have lost our home, Emma, to the insurgents. He cannot return to the Pavilion. But we have arranged to rendezvous at the Café Tabac in the Rue Poland, where my father can take sanctuary with Sigi Lasard. He will stay in the hostel for a while, until he can contact other members of the Golden Clasp and make arrangements to continue his own fight for the future of France.'

'He will be safe, Armand. I feel sure of it,' Emma assured him.

'Believe me, we shall work together for what we believe is a better future for our country,' affirmed Armand.

Emma and Armand paused now and Armand said, 'We have not spoken of our own future, Emma, but I believe we shall unite our lives and make our own future together in time.'

'I believe that, too,' answered Emma.

'I pledge myself to you,' said Armand.

'My pledge is to you also, Armand.'

They kissed then, and held each other tightly. Both knew that this was a solemn moment for them, as they stood together on the dockside, amid ropes, barrels of tar and ships lined up along the quay.

Yvette seemed brighter as they stepped aboard the packet. She said an affectionate goodbye to Philippe and he to her. She said to Emma, 'It has happened so quickly. So rapidly. I can scarcely believe it. One moment I was mourning the betrayal of Carlo, and the next Philippe has entered my life! We plan to meet again. We have so much in common. It is a miracle, Emma. A shaft of good fortune for us both! Love at first sight!'

So chatting, the two friends went below to their cabin. Later, on deck, they were not surprised to see the second officer of the ship, again.

'I remember you, sir!' cried Yvette. 'You were forward in your suggestions to us when we sailed with you before! But now you see before you two ladies who are betrothed. Or almost. Spoken for, at least. We will stand no nonsense from you this time, sir. So please do not waste your flirtatious comments upon us.'

At Dover, Emma was able to hire a carriage to take them to Little Marlowe. And so they journeyed through the English countryside, towards her home.

As they approached the Bell House, Emma was surprised to see that everything looked the same.

So much had happened to her, so many momentous events had taken place in her life since she had left home, she had almost expected to find some difference in her familiar surroundings.

But the drive was the same, the garden, the house still stood square and solid in the sunlight. A great wave of happiness and expectation swept over her at the prospect of seeing her father again, of sleeping in her own room, of eating English food and pursuing her usual happy and useful routine.

Emma sprang from the carriage and rushed into the house, followed slowly by Yvette. But to her surprise the hallway was silent. The house seemed still. She walked along the corridor and entered the study.

Her father was seated at his desk, surrounded by his usual pile of papers and books. She saw his face light up when he saw her. He rose to his feet and moved to clasp her in his arms.

'Emma! You have returned! I thought never to see you again! I thought you had perished in the revolution, but you are here. Now! And also Yvette!'

They sat around the fireside and Lizbeth brought in very welcome refreshments. Then Emma asked the question which was in the forefront of her mind. 'Where is Mrs Kent? I mean, my step-mother, Father! She is absent. Where is she?'

'She has left me, Emma. Deserted myself and the household. She went to visit her sister in Brighton and there she has remained. There are balls there, entertainments, card parties and the like.

She believes she has entered society! I am sure she will not return.'

Emma and Yvette now entered into the calm and pleasant atmosphere of the Bell House. Emma found her father had fallen behind with his work for the university. And she was once more busy writing up his notes, adding up the students' accounts and keeping his diary up to date.

Yvette at first helped Lizbeth, the housekeeper, but later she began a small school in the village. She was well remembered before for her tuition in deportment, and pupils of all ages were soon to be enrolled in her thriving academy.

News filtered through to the household from France. Philippe and Maître Barre had removed Henri from the orphanage and had taken him into their own home. This was an informal adoption which was to benefit all three.

King Louis XVI was executed by the guillotine on the 21st January 1793. And Queen Marie Antoinette followed on the 16th October 1793. These executions were a matter of great rejoicing to the revolutionaries and their followers. But many in France had second thoughts.

They felt themselves diminished by these deaths. And they felt their country, France, was diminished also.

'There is no doubt the common people of France had right on their side, in this civil war,' commented the professor. 'But they defeated their own ends by their cruelty and violence. Indeed, in a way, nothing will change. At the end of this internal conflict, matters will return to normal. Almost to the state where they had been before.

'And what is to follow? Napoleon Bonaparte is flexing his muscles and eyeing up the country he wishes to call his own. He is considering the possibilities and planning his strategy. Another venture which will appear triumphant but which will end in disaster! But these are only my own opinions,' stated the professor. 'History, alone, will prove me right or wrong. And the French people the same.

'The Golden Clasp!' cried the professor finally. 'The hand of friendship! Would that this were evident throughout the world!'

Henri wrote to Emma when communications were possible. He was happy and successful in his studies of the law, and

212

within the household of the Barre family.

Later, when France had returned to stability and lands and properties were restored to their rightful owners, the Château Duval was returned to Henri. He was decreed to be the new Count Duval, for his father and mother were never traced amid the vortex of the revolution. They were only two of the citizens, both high and low, who vanished at this time.

Though only in his teens, Henri proved himself a resourceful and kindly manager of the château and its estates. He seemed mature beyond his years, as were all who lived through those days of oppression and persecution.

But history? Emma and Yvette did not look so far ahead; nor did they look back. Emma had, perhaps, helped to make history. But for now, she was devoted to her own studies and her pleasant way of life.

Emma and Yvette had their own personal matters to consider. For they had heard that Armand and Philippe would be visiting England in the spring, to lay before the British Parliament the aims and progress of the Golden Clasp.

Good news, indeed! They would be guests at the Bell House. It seemed that better fortune was on the way; happiness was, at last, within reach of them all.

Historical Note

While it is generally supposed that the French Revolution was a conflict of citizens, yet it had within its core several conflicting elements, each party striving for supremacy, gain or revenge.

The Revolution began in 1789 with the storming of the Bastille by revolutionary forces. Then followed the death by guillotine of the aristocratic offenders, which rapidly degenerated into hatred and destruction of ordinary citizens who opposed the ruling circle.

After 1793, the climax of the Revolution was reached with the death of King Louis XVI and Queen Marie Antoinette. While many citizens regarded this as a logical triumph of the uprising, others had second thoughts, and from this time the power of the Revolution declined.

The uprising ended in 1795, the year in which Napoleon Bonaparte prepared the conquest of the Italians. So began another era of doubt and conflict to assail the citizens of the beautiful and historic country of France.

We do hope that you have enjoyed reading this large print book.

Did you know that all of our titles are available for purchase?

We publish a wide range of high quality large print books including:
Romances, Mysteries, Classics
General Fiction
Non Fiction and Western

Special interest titles available in large print are:
The Little Oxford Dictionary
Music Book, Song Book
Hymn Book, Service Book

Also available from us courtesy of Oxford University Press:
Young Readers' Dictionary
(large print edition)
Young Readers' Thesaurus
(large print edition)

For further information or a free brochure, please contact us at:
Ulverscroft Large Print Books Ltd.,
The Green, Bradgate Road, Anstey,
Leicester, LE7 7FU, England.
Tel: (00 44) **0116 236 4325**
Fax: (00 44) **0116 234 0205**

THE WILDEST DREAM

Kirsty White

Roscawl, July 1848

My dearest Michael,

I do not know when we can meet again.

My father discovered I stole food to give to the villagers who are starving since the potato famine. Now I am banished to my room, and who knows when I will be set free.

And now they are planning to marry me to a useless fop called Edward Cavendish. But I will not. I will not.

Michael, can you wait for me? Together we WILL find a way. We must . . .

Elizabeth